DIAGNOSIS: MURDER

THE LT. VALCOUR SERIES

DIAGNOSIS: MURDER

ADVENTURES IN CRIME WITH
DR. COLIN STARR, M.D.

RUFUS KING

WILDSIDE PRESS

CONTENTS

THE CASE OF THE THREE BALEFUL BROTHERS

Furs relieved her face from looking negligent, two handsome pelts of soft blue fox, while an effective French hat set off dark hair of an unexciting brown. Only the young woman's fine eyes seemed vital, and they were activated by a gripping, a profound sense of fear. She was young. She would be twenty-two next month, on the eleventh of May.

She left Onega Drive and turned her car in between entrance gates, on one of which a small, severely plain sign read: Colin Starr, M.D. She drew up before a mansion, the spacious unrailed verandas of which were more suitable to a plantation than to southeastern Ohio. It was an ugly, a substantial house, built in the days of Dr. Starr's father when solid mass (without the least condescension toward line) spelled substance. Its two high stories were crowned by the reluctant awkwardness of a mansard roof and it, in turn, was knobbed by a cupola from where a magnificent view of the Onega River and the surrounding hills and town of Laurel Falls could be obtained but never was.

Miss Wadsworth, Starr's secretary, opened the heavy oak door. You felt a starched white severity in Miss Wadsworth, a guardian quality: one in defense against any frittering away of moments which should be fortressed against all but the most pressing things. The young woman's eyes shocked her.

She said, "Good morning, Miss Shepmann. I'm afraid the doctor's appointments don't start for several hours. He could see you, I think, just after two."

Eleanore Shepmann's gloved hands were trembling.

"It isn't that, Miss Wadsworth. I'm not ill."

"No?"

"May I come in?"

"Forgive me. Of course."

The heavy oak door closed, shutting out pale April sunlight which hinted at storm, leaving the large hallway cool and very quiet and dim.

"You haven't heard?"

"Heard what, Miss Shepmann? The doctor has been dictating all morning. He is reading a paper tomorrow in Columbus on blood dyscrasias."

"Milton Forstair has been shot to death."

Miss Wadsworth looked at her sharply.

"My dear child, you *are* ill. Sit here. Wait."

Miss Wadsworth moved swiftly through a reception room, through another doorway and into an office furnished with an agreeable simplicity. The doctor looked up from across a rosewood desk and she felt that exciting sense of a magnetic virility which was there whenever Starr's eyes turned suddenly upon you, making you forget the all but ungainly planes of his strong body and of his features, which were not quite ugly.

"Miss Eleanore Shepmann is here, Doctor. Her fiancé, Mr. Milton Forstair, has been shot. He is dead."

His expression changed a little, almost as though the news were not news but rather a period mark to a sentence which he had believed conceivable for quite some time. He asked Miss Wadsworth to show Miss Shepmann in. He went to a cabinet and started to mix, in a glass, an anodyne for nervous shock.

He knew Eleanore Shepmann well, also her three brothers: Humphrey, Walter and Douglas, with the somewhat sinister facades and viperish manner of tongue which it pleased the young men to present to the world. He knew, too, the glamorous Milton Forstair who had been Eleanore's fiancé and who now was violently dead.

He was (Forstair) an importation from the caviar-and-Courvoisier intellectuals of New York and had been lured to Laurel Falls by a Mrs. Selldon Poole to hatch her latest movement: a community theater. One production had occurred to date, an elegant spy affair, larded with military secrets and revolvers and tinged, Starr had thought, with pseudo-Chekhov and the more depressing aspects of international sex.

He recalled the reports of Forstair's arrival, which had galvanized the social nerve centers of the town over two months back. Trunks, suitcases, shoe and hat boxes in assorted calf, linen and pigskin had held the young Apollo's collection of knockouts from wine-toned dinner jackets to absolutely rugged tweeds. Edna Poole had attended to Forstair's temperamental passion for privacy by installing him aboard her husband's houseboat, *Buckeye II*, which was moored to the dock of their estate on Onega Drive. Forstair had there, presumably, communed in peace on the bosom of the river, with all catering and maid service supplied from the house.

Edna's husband, Selldon Poole, had accepted this installation with the same almost patrician courtesy with which he had become accustomed to accept, for the past several years, Edna's assortment of energetic enthusiasms and, alternatively, depressive moods. Edna was his second wife and had been met, the town understood, during a Southern cruise aboard *Buckeye II* in Florida waters. Her background, the town also understood, was Aiken and New Jersey.

Selldon Poole's first wife had died a decade ago, leaving him a son Jeffry, who was now twenty-five: a healthy and wholesomely pleasant young man with a stolid interest in polo, golf, Gaspe salmon expeditions and very little else. In common with the rest of the country-club crowd Starr had always taken it for granted that Jeffry Poole and Eleanore Shepmann would marry, whenever Jeffry could get his mind off sport for long enough to suggest it. They had grown up together, and the Shepmann and Poole estates touched.

The glittering invasion of Milton Forstair had, however, blasted all that.

Starr went to Eleanore as she came into the office. He took her hand. He attempted to readjust his viewpoint of her under this new light reflected from murder. She had never occurred to him as apt for the role of a *femme fatale* against whom the more emotional waves of life would break violently. That still struck him as nonsense. Her attributes remained unchanged: a pleasant, girl-scout face and the Shepmann money. There was a lot of money, and it had been in the children's own control since their parents' death. He handed her a glass.

"Drink this, Eleanore."

"Thank you, Doctor."

He asked her to sit down. He stood beside her and said with a grave, curiously old-fashioned courtesy, "What can I do?"

"They think that my brothers did it. I could tell that, Doctor, from the things that District Attorney Heffernan asked me."

The distaste of the three Shepmann boys for the engagement between Eleanore and Forstair had been open and poisonous ever since the engagement had been announced early last week.

Starr said, "Just tell me."

"It's so unfair—I mean, simply because there were so many shots… you've helped others in cases like this, Doctor—I hoped that somehow you would help my brothers—help me—"

She started to tremble, to cry, and he saw it was no use. It would be a good ten minutes before the sedative would quiet her nerves from their brutal shock. He rang for Miss Wadsworth. He asked her to stay with Eleanore. He went into the reception room and dialed a desk phone. He asked to speak with District Attorney Heffernan.

Heffernan was exact.

Milton Forstair had been found dead at nine o'clock that morning by the maid who had brought his breakfast down to the houseboat. His bed had been slept in. He was wearing a tweed suit. An overcoat and hat were thrown on a sofa. A packed suitcase stood beside the sofa. Forstair had died on the floor of the main cabin. He had been shot seven times.

The coroner had extracted the bullets and had established the damning fact that they had come from three guns of different calibers: a .25 automatic Colt, a .32 Smith & Wesson Long, a 7.63 Mauser.

Heffernan said that the fact was damning insofar as the three Shepmann brothers were concerned. The Shepmann family had originated in Tennessee, atavistic (if Starr wished) to feuds, to a removal in the grand manner—the brothers had simply reverted to the habits of their forebears, had got out their guns and had pumped lead. Not, Heffernan pointed out, that the case rested on the gun angle alone.

Starr asked on what else.

There seemed to be plenty. In addition to the generally known hatred on the brothers' part for Milton Forstair there had been specific threats. Douglas Shepmann had stated at the yacht-club bar on Saturday that he would remove Forstair's liver and fry it before he would let any velour-lined G-boy marry his sister. Humphrey had specified tweezers, while Walter, the youngest, had gone into detail about asps.

Starr contended that the threats were perfectly in character and just so much wind blown out for effect.

"I'd agree with you, Colin," Heffernan said, "except for the circumstances of last night. Forstair was killed around midnight, say half an hour's leeway either way. Well, none of the Shepmann boys has been seen since an hour before that time."

"They're missing?"

"They couldn't be more so. We know that Humphrey Shepmann left a poker game at the Downtown Club at eleven. He looked at his watch and said that he and his brothers had 'something to attend to.' He cashed in his chips and left. He left, according to old Colonel Wattrous, in a blasted hurry and looking like a mad tiger about to pull off a job. The colonel's own words, Colin."

"The colonel had probably been a heavy loser."

"Perhaps. Take Walter Shepmann. He was last seen at half-past ten at the bar of that pesthole run by Spinelli. He was, according to Spinelli, awash with scotch. His eyebrows formed a black lead pipe. Appropriate muscles twitched in his colorless face and he patted a hip pocket significantly. I'll grant you some rear-view propheticism, but Spinelli swears that the pocket housed a gun."

"Personally I suspect a flask. And I admire Spinelli's imagery, if nothing else about him."

"The official mind still favors the gun. Walter also looked at his watch, commented on the hour, and Spinelli has him leaving the bar with 'murder hot in each eye.'"

"Which is just so much Sicilian histrionics."

"We prefer to think not. Finally, take Douglas Shepmann. *He* was last seen at a quarter to eleven running for the main exit of the Bijoux, where that sea film is playing. The one where everybody sinks but Tyrone Power. Douglas knocked an usher down on the way. Evidently the usher had repressions. He simply said that 'Mr. Shepmann had seemed distrait.'"

"And that's your case?"

"It is to date, and it's enough, isn't it?"

Starr admitted that it was. The whole pattern was in keeping with the Shepmann brothers' flair for the dramatic, with their utter disregard for the consequences of anything that was ever said or done. He admitted there was no sound reason why warrants should not have been issued for their arrest: the charge, murder. He thanked Heffernan and hung up.

Eleanore was better. Her nerves were under control, but there still was a certain bright and unreal quality in her manner which puzzled Starr and made him suspect that she was holding herself on guard.

He said, after Miss Wadsworth had left them, "Where are your brothers, Eleanore? You know, don't you?"

Her smile continued strangely bright.

"Yes. I wouldn't tell the police, but I'll tell you."

"All right."

"I wired them about Milton. I got an answer just before coming here. They said, 'Let us be the first to congratulate you.' They wouldn't, they *couldn't* have sent that sort of a message if they'd shot Milton, Doctor." (Unfortunately, Starr thought, they most certainly could.) "They're flying back."

"From where?"

"From New York. They took a plane from Columbus at two o'clock last night." Forstair was shot close on midnight; the brothers were last seen at eleven; their time between then and two o'clock was so far unaccounted for—more grist for Heffernan's mill, Starr thought.

"Why did they fly to New York, Eleanore?"

"To stop the elopement, Doctor."

"Of you and Milton?"

"Yes. They were so horrid about the engagement that Milton and I decided to elope and sort of get it over with. They couldn't have been more beastly, Doctor, more pig-headed. They were convinced that Milton was simply marrying me for my money."

Starr said carefully, "There were others who thought that too, Eleanore."

"I know. I didn't care about them, but I did care about my brothers. Milton had money. He carried a checking balance of five thousand with the First National here in town and one of fifteen thousand with the Merchants Trust in New York."

"He told you that?"

"No, Doctor. He insisted on proving it. He knew how the boys felt. He brought them certified statements from both managers. They—well, the boys simply insisted that he did it with mirrors and that they disliked him for his tweeds anyhow."

"How did they find out about the elopement?"

"Through Douglas. He's always been an awful sneak. He's so perfectly barefaced about it. I mean he'll steam open the flaps of envelopes and then won't even bother to seal them up again. Milton said that my last note hadn't been resealed. I should have known that Douglas had steamed it. If I hadn't been so excited about everything I would have."

"It discussed your plans for the elopement?"

"Yes, and it mentioned the Ambassador as where we'd stay in New York. That's where I wired them. I was to meet Milton at the Columbus airport at half-past one for the night plane. That's how I happened to be there when the boys drove in at two and chartered a Boeing job to chase me to New York. I kept out of sight. They didn't see me."

And still, Starr thought, no alibi. The Shepmanns could well have gone to the houseboat and blasted Forstair before setting out for Columbus. Their subsequent flight to New York to prevent an elopement with a prospective bridegroom who was already a corpse was thoroughly in keeping with what they would have devised as a bright and macabre false trail.

Eleanore's smile, with its quick, artificial strain, was suddenly gone, and her voice tightened as she said, "I decided Milton knew the boys had found out about the elopement and that he had therefore decided to call it off. I drove back. I kept thinking on the way that possibly they'd gone to the houseboat and possibly—well, thrashed Milton."

"In that case why would they have taken a plane to New York?"

"I don't know. It's—not having the answer to that is what's been frightening me so. Perhaps they thought I'd gone on alone. I don't know, Doctor."

"Perhaps. When did you get home?"

"Around four. I put the car in the garage. I took the path along the river over to the Poole dock."

"Do the police know this?"

"No. Nobody does, Doctor."

"You found Milton shot?"

"I didn't go into the cabin. I looked inside through a porthole. The ceiling lights were on." She said, with a dreadful sort of earnestness, "I—anybody could have told he was dead."

"Did you love him, Eleanore? Really?"

"I don't know. I don't know what love is. I thought I knew, but I'm no longer sure. It was like something hitting you when you first met Milton, not a physical thing but more like a light, such a blinding light that it kept you from seeing anything else." She looked at him helplessly and said, "The thing is it's gone, whatever it was I felt for Milton. Is it stupid to believe that it, too, was killed when he was killed? You know about those things, Doctor."

"I sometimes fool myself into thinking I do. Then it just adds up into a general knowledge, which is rarely helpful for any specific case."

"I know. You have to do your own spring cleaning if it's to be a good job." He was glad she saw it like that. House cleaning, wiping off the slate, the terms didn't matter. The thing was, she'd be in shape soon to realize her love for Jeffry Poole again, unexciting, perhaps, but right and lasting. He thought her ever so lucky that Forstair was dead before disillusionment had come, as it would have, souring her entire life and blunting her abilities to feel things with the honesty and zest of youth.

He said, "What's really troubling you, Eleanore?"

She stared at him earnestly.

"There's no earthly sense in not being completely honest with you, telling you everything."

"None. If I'm to help you."

She took a silver cigarette lighter from her bag.

"This was on the deck. I gave it to Plumphrey last Christmas."

He left it lying on the desk where she had placed it.

"I shall have to tell Mr. Heffernan all of this, Eleanore."

"Yes, I thought that. I wanted you to know first, to know everything, Doctor."

"I'll do everything I can."

"Does it—is it all pretty grim?"

He smiled at her gravely.

"Yes. Pretty grim."

* * * *

The police photographs of the scene of the crime were good. One close-up of the body interested Starr especially. It showed Forstair flat on his back on the cabin deck. It was a view from the waist up, in excellent focus. The left arm was twisted and partially hidden beneath the body. The right arm was crooked, with its hand and fingers rigid and held, through an after-death muscular contraction, about a foot away from the body. It had then been fixed there by rigor mortis. A dark speck showed in the center of the back of the hand.

Rain started falling as Starr drove to the mortuary and viewed the body itself. Its classical beauty was out of key, as if life's guards were down. A touch of petulance, of greed pinched the full, clear-cut lips, and sea-blue eyes were fogged dull with ash. Magnificent physique remained, that and a crop of naturally curly chestnut hair. Yes, Starr imagined, a girl could be struck blind by a getup like that. There was an insensate fury in the way the body had been riddled. Starr studied the pattern of wounds. He identified the black speck in the police photograph as one where a bullet had first passed through the right hand before it had entered the chest; rigor mortis still obtained, and the line of fire of that shot was obvious. He looked at the coroner's notes and studied the angles which the courses of the other bullets had taken. He thanked the attendant and left the mortuary.

Rain fell harder and the sky was a murky gray as he got into his black sedan and drove slowly through the business section of the town to Onega Drive. He turned south along the river, thinking that in its waters the three murder guns would be lying. He supposed a diver would be sent down to look near the houseboat and the Poole dock. The hard bottom would not conceal them, unless they had been cast beyond retrieve into the whirlpool at the base of the falls to the north.

That small black dot, which was directly in the line of fire—

A wave of heat surged through him, then left him cold. His thoughts, the picture which they saw, appalled him. He concentrated sharply on each facet of a death by gunfire, marshaled the minutiae of his own experiences and of the cases about which he had read. He increased the car's speed. The town's great estates flashed by until he reached the massive entrance gates to the Pooles'. He saw, as he had expected, District Attorney Heffernan's coupe and a police car parked down by the river alongside the dock, where the deckhouse and superstructure of *Buckeye II* was visible through the rain and trees. He saw Eleanore Shepmann's Mercedes in the large parking space before the handsome pillared portico of the house. Off to the left of the house, across a great space of lawn, he saw the large barn which Edna Poole (and Selldon Poole's checkbook) had converted into the charming theater where Milton Forstair's genius had incubated in a blissful state of carte blanche.

He took a right-hand fork in the driveway and went down to the dock. He boarded *Buckeye II* and joined Heffernan on the afterdeck. Heffernan was pleased.

He pointed to a lumped cloth on the deck and said, "We've had luck. That's the Colt and the Mauser. Jock's after the Smith and Wesson now."

Starr watched the bullet head and seal torso of a man break water and gulp air before submerging again.

He said to Heffernan, "I want to talk to you. There's something you ought to know."

He gave a detailed résumé of Eleanore Shepmann's visit. He gave Heffernan the silver cigarette lighter. He described his visit to the mortuary and the appalling deductions he had drawn.

Heffernan looked bleak.

"I see. Another one of those."

"I'm afraid it is."

"Look here, Colin—those guns. I mean you can't just walk out nowadays and pick guns up."

"I've thought of that. There wasn't any need to. You saw the spy play which Forstair put on. There must have been five or six guns at least among its props."

"Of course." Heffernan repeated it slowly, "Of course..."

The bullet-headed seal came up with the Smith & Wesson, and Heffernan added it to the other two. Then he talked some more with Starr. Fingerprints, he said, were out. *Buckeye II* was littered with them, with everybody's. What could they do? Starr spoke of traps, of one in especial that had been set to catch a thief. There was a way.

He suggested that arrangements for arresting the Shepmann brothers on their arrival at the Columbus airport be done by telephone from the Poole house and done in a manner so that Eleanore, who was there, would know about it. He suggested that Heffernan, from a private telephone, make five local calls. He wrote on the back of an envelope the data which should be used during the local calls. He looked at his watch. It was a quarter to one.

He said, "Shall we go up to the house? It's just before lunch. They ought to be together now."

* * * *

Medcalf, the manservant who opened the door, looked stringy. He took their hats and coats, glanced with vague reproach at Heffernan and then said to Starr: "It's been a shock, Doctor. The staff's upset. Alice has been having them ever since she found him, off and on. Mrs. Alcott's been giving her ammonia and burning feathers."

Starr translated this accurately as that Alice was the maid who had discovered the body and had been having intermittent hysterics for which the cook had been applying old-time simples. He shook a couple of pills from a phial in a pocket case and gave them to Medcalf.

"Give her these. If she isn't better let me know."

"Thank you, Doctor. I will."

The living room was saturated with Edna Poole's mood of last winter, which had veered suddenly from Empire to American Chippendale because of a stunning secretary bookcase (block-front interior, leaded glass, 1760) which she had been permitted to "discover" in a Madison Avenue shop in New York at the tempting price of twelve hundred dollars.

They were at cocktails: Edna and Selldon Poole, Jeffry Poole and Eleanore Shepmann. A pre-lunch necessity this time, Edna said, rather than a gesture, due to the morning's tragedy and the general state of nerves. The atmosphere was not comfortable. Starr sensed the hidden piling up of lightnings, stored for later discharge.

He thought that Selldon Poole had a shrunken look, as if his years (he was fifty-seven) had suddenly moved in and made him shrivel. Selldon was a small man anyhow and seemed, in consequence, to carry every inch with a careful and great dignity. Jeffry was a good four inches taller than his father and much more solid. His eyes were desperately worried. He couldn't keep them away from Eleanore, who was a wreck.

Edna Poole alone was controlled and, Starr thought, curiously detached. Her voice, when she greeted him and Heffernan, had seemed tuned, quite low and sultry like a humid summer twilight. They refused cocktails, and Heffernan apologized for bothering but asked whether he might use the telephone. He wanted to call the airport and the police department in Columbus. Edna said, through the sudden chill silence, that there was a phone in the coatroom off the entrance hall.

Heffernan hesitated in the doorway. He said, "By the way, did any of you hear the shots last night?"

Selldon Poole said thoughtfully, "We couldn't have, Mr. Heffernan. The boat's too far away."

"Yes, I suppose it is. You were here around midnight, Mr. Poole?"

"No, as a matter of fact I was not. I got home around two. Jeffry picked me up at the office and drove me home. I was preparing a brief on the Drochmann case." Heffernan stared thoughtfully at Jeffry, then said, "Were you here at midnight, Mr. Poole?"

"No, I was planning a fishing trip with Jim Tanner until after eleven, then I just drove around until it was time to pick up Father."

Heffernan smiled faintly.

"I'm afraid you're my last hope, Mrs. Poole."

She smiled back and said, "Yes, I was here, Mr. Heffernan. But I heard no shots."

"Thank you."

Heffernan left the room, and Eleanore went to Starr swiftly and said, "They'll be arrested when they land?"

"Yes."

"There was nothing you could do?"

Starr answered her hesitantly. "I suggested the *moulage* test. Of course it's a negative one at best."

"*Moulage?*"

"For powder grains. When you shoot a revolver, especially if the breech is at all defective, the backflash imbeds traces of powder into the skin around the base of the thumb. The *moulage* is some sort of a plastelline substance they press on the skin. It collects the powder traces so that they can be tested and identified."

Selldon Poole said, "But surely they'll have washed their hands?"

"Washing has no effect on the powder traces, Mr. Poole. They're too deeply embedded. Only some solvent, like bromophenol, can remove them."

Eleanore said swiftly, "Bromophenol, Doctor?"

"Yes. It's a powder itself, a pale yellowish stuff. You rub it on the skin and let it stay for a couple of hours, and the gunpowder traces are gone." His voice softened, became oddly gentle. "It's all right your knowing about it, Eleanore. I'm not going behind Mr. Heffernan's back. He's arranging that your brothers be given the *moulage* test by the Columbus police as soon as they land."

* * * *

By three o'clock the storm was at its height. Rain fell in torrents, and the sky was the color of lead. The Shepmann brothers were aboard *Buckeye II*, being questioned by the police. They had been escorted from Columbus by motorcycle outriders with, to their intense satisfaction, screaming sirens. Eleanore and Jeffry and Selldon Poole were aboard with them.

Edna Poole had remained in the house. In a mood.

Starr stood for a moment in the living-room doorway and looked at Edna. She was over by a window, staring through the sheeting rain across lawns toward the dock, a vague figure, dark in the room's dusk.

"Mrs. Poole."

She turned slowly.

"Oh—you, Doctor."

"Medcalf said I would find you in here."

"Yes?"

He joined her at the window, stood near her and felt an unwilling admiration for the placidity of her features, for the calmness of her breathing.

She said after a while, "You wanted something, Doctor?"

"A confession, Mrs. Poole."

She thought this over, studied his face.

"Of what?"

"Confession is perhaps the wrong word. A confirmation of your motive would be more exact."

"Motive?"

"For having killed Mr. Forstair."

Rain against glass was the only sound for several moments.

"Shall we sit down, Doctor?"

"Certainly."

She arranged herself in an armchair. Her hands were dim and quiet on her lap in the room's deep shadow. She said, "That's an extraordinary thing to say. It's so absurd—well, it stifles any normal reaction. I never realized that you had a sense of humor. One in such bad taste."

"Was it because of the use to which Mr. Forstair put the twenty thousand dollars?"

The pale hands clenched and then were quiet again. She said nothing.

Starr went on: "I don't know what hold Mr. Forstair had over you. It doesn't matter. I should imagine it must have been something that happened in the East. But it must have been strong enough to have caused you to give him that lump sum. I suppose the money came from Mr. Poole's marriage settlement?"

"This is just as insulting as it is stupid, Doctor."

"No, not stupid. I think it quite clear and quite in keeping with what your reactions would be."

"Reactions?"

"You were more than just in love with Mr. Forstair. You were infatuated with him. You couldn't help being so, no matter whether he were blackmailing you or not. No matter whether some hold he had over you jeopardized your position here, your home." He added gently, "You see—well, with women of your age, Mrs. Poole..."

Her voice was instantly sharp.

"At my age?"

"At forty, possibly a few years more. As I say, the method or reason he used for getting the money is of no consequence. I'm certain, however, that his having used it to lull Eleanore Shepmann's suspicions that he was a fortune hunter drove you off balance, Mrs. Poole."

She said with deadly restraint, "You appreciate that this is slanderous libel?"

"No, it's the truth. An insane jealousy, the depth to which Mr. Forstair had hurt you, your feeling of having been cruelly betrayed, all of those things made you plan and execute his murder. They made you do so in such a way that the Shepmann family would fall within your vengeance."

Her laugh, with its attempt at derision, was unsure.

"Have you forgotten that the case is ended? There were three guns. There are three Shepmann brothers. Their motive for the murder is obvious. They have no alibis whatsoever for—midnight, wasn't it, when the shots were fired?"

"But they weren't fired at midnight, Mrs. Poole."

Her immense calm persisted. She said quietly, "I understand the coroner has established that they were."

"No, he established the fact that Mr. Forstair died some time in the neighborhood of midnight."

"Well?"

"He died at midnight from a single shot which passed directly through his heart. The other shots, at the very earliest, were fired into his dead body over two hours later. They were definitely fired after two o'clock. The Shepmann brothers do have alibis for then."

She said almost academically, "I think it is you who have—lost balance, Doctor. If a bullet were to break a watch, stop it at a certain hour, that I could understand."

"One of the bullets did better than that. It passed through the back of a hand, on its way to the body, *after that hand had been set rigid by rigor mortis.*"

"Interesting." Her voice held a sudden edge. She made an effort to control herself and said, "You will understand when I ask you to leave this house? To leave it now?"

Starr did not move. He said patiently, "You must have known about the proposed elopement. I suppose Mr. Forstair simply told you. He would have been perfectly sure of himself, quite sure about the strength of his hold over you. I think that the first shot unnerved you, the shot that killed him. It was passion that lay dying on the floor before you, not just a man. I think you fled back here, blindly, to the shelter of your room and that it was several hours later before you were able to get yourself in hand sufficiently to return to the boat and fire the other guns, in order to complete your plan. That much you did know, that bullets were extracted and their calibers determined. Just when did you get hold of Humphrey Shepmann's silver cigarette lighter?"

"At the country—get out of here!" She was shrill, no longer a poised sultry twilight but gratingly harsh and shrill. "Get out! Get out!"

Still he did not move.

"Mrs. Poole, there was a trap once laid to catch a thief. Coins were being stolen from clothing in the lockers of a school. So they coated some coins with a powder, and the thief took them, and after a while his nerves, his fear of detection, perhaps his conscience if you wish, caused him to sweat, and the sweat reacted upon the pale yellow powder on his finger tips and turned them a bright blue."

He heard her draw one quick sharp breath.

He said, "As you've realized the name of that powder was blue of bromophenol. Mr. Heffernan arranged with the five druggists in town that anyone telephoning or calling for bromophenol be given it and that he be notified. He was. He arranged that your husband and Jeffry and Eleanore be down at the houseboat so that you would be alone when I came here. I must retract what I said here before lunch. Bromophenol has no reaction whatever upon traces of gunpowder. But it does retain its virtues as a trap."

He reached swiftly for the cord of a standing lamp and pulled it. It's light shafted whitely on flesh, at the base of the thumb of her right hand where a gun would backfire, on the skin's vivid blue.

There was pathos in her crumpling, as when anything that is sure and strong and vital suddenly succumbs to a swift decay, and to the frailty of her voice as she sent it with a desperate, heartfelt urgency toward that ultimate appeal: "…God…dearest God…"

Starr placed his hand over hers, covering with a gentle strength the betraying blue, feeling her a woman again whose soul was sick, and brain.

He said, "Is it all right for Mr. Heffernan to come in, Mrs. Poole? Will you tell him now?"

She clung to his hand. She held it very tight. She said, "Oh *yes.*"

THE CASE OF THE PRODIGAL BRIDEGROOM

Midway between the Prairie Plains and the Allegheny Plateau, there in the state of Ohio, snug in its southeastern rugged land and hills, secure on the banks of the Muskingum River, the city of Laurel Falls and its seventy thousand odd souls faced with commonplace serenity the evening of June twenty-second.

Dr. Colin Starr permitted his car to drift. He continued to feel a sense of irritation that his dinner and bridge at the Haverings' should be interrupted by a stomach-ache.

Miss Wadsworth, his secretary, had relayed the simple symptoms of a mild indigestion when the call had come in, with the request that Dr. Starr stop at the Arthur Chanin house and see Mr. Chanin at his, Dr. Starr's, convenience. Mrs. Chanin, Miss Wadsworth had said, had telephoned herself: Her husband had begun to feel indisposed shortly under an hour ago, a mild nausea, slight cramps, possibly something injudicious at luncheon, so if Dr. Starr wouldn't mind?

Starr smiled faintly as he pictured the tone of voice which Edna Chanin would have used: cool, unhurried and, yes, ineffably gracious, just as her whole attitude toward Laurel Falls had been gracious since Arthur Chanin had brought her home from New York as a bride six years ago. A curious woman, Starr thought her, playing a role so meticulously that it had become the real thing. Precisely what that role had masked he did not know. Nor did the country-club crowd know, nor the town's backstairs tribunals. They, he knew, she had passed with flying colors, for servants thought her "ever so nice" and (in comparison with some of the town's matrons who might be mentioned and were) a "lady."

Starr wondered idly at the odd impulse which had impelled him to break up the opening rubber of bridge and start for the Chanins' at once. Certainly there had been nothing alarming in the symptoms which Miss Wadsworth had relayed him, but there it was.

There were three Chanins: Arthur and his wife Edna and Arthur's younger brother Robert. Starr's card file on each was clinically unexceptional. Arthur Chanin's digestive system was chronically out of tone from over-rich foods and a sedentary habit of living. His sole occupation in life consisted of being a gentleman and a scholar, and the pursuit enthralled him.

Edna Chanin had come to him in March and had delicately instructed him in the facts of life to a point where he had finally grasped the idea that she expected to have a baby. This he had confirmed, and the child was scheduled to take over the Chanin torch sometime in December.

Robert Chanin was an alcoholic, his entire system shot, and with an unpredictable but presumably brief span left him to live.

Beyond the clinical, however, there were (on Starr's card files) certain brief annotations. On Arthur Chanin's: Smiles without humor; not miserly, but has a dementia toward pennies.

On Robert Chanin's: Needs a Holy Grail. Starr did not know exactly why he had jotted the phrase down, but it did comprise in a sort of concentrated-pill form his feelings about the youngster, his feeling that if Robert Chanin had lived in the era of Crusades he would not have been the wastrel that he was today.

On Edna Chanin's: Why take swimming lessons when she knows how to swim? That had been the previous summer (long before she had tactfully led him through the mazes of her currently scheduled blessed event) and it had puzzled him until he had seen the new swimming instructor at the River Club: something blond out of Norway with a Hollywood build, and Edna Chanin had started with the breast stroke, then graduated, with astonishing rapidity, into an Australian crawl.

Starr turned into the Chanin driveway, heard the sing of crushed gravel for fifty yards, admired, as he always did, an impressive row of coster blue spruces on his right, then drew up before the handsome limestone facade of the house itself. The June air was redolent with moist greens, and twilight gave way to stars and the first deep dark of night as he mounted shallow steps and pressed a bell.

He said, "Hello, Maxwell," to the manservant who opened the door.

"Good evening, Doctor."

"How are the twinges?"

"Much better since the pills."

"Let me know when you need more."

"Thank you."

Maxwell took Starr's hat and gloves and coat. He carried them into a small room that opened out of the ponderous elegance of the large entrance hall, and Edna Chanin was starting down the dark mahogany stairs just as Starr reached the base of them. Light from the hall's great luster chandelier heightened the pallor of her face, with its dark direct eyes and madonna cap of sleek dark hair, and it occurred to Starr that she was more impressively beautiful than he had ever before thought, and that age (he knew her to be in her thirties) had not touched her at all.

Her hand was cool and her grip firmly assured. She said, "Before you go up, Doctor?"

Her smile, conservatively tinged with worry, made her utterly charming. A scent of the perfume which had knocked them dead at the club's May Day dance stirred as she passed him, and he followed her into the dim privacy of a small room.

They sat on gilt and tapestry, and she said, "It's beyond a slight attack of indigestion this time, Doctor." She studied briefly the intelligence and virility which saved Starr's features from being handsome. "Do you mind my discussing it?"

He accepted the inevitable and said, "Of course not."

"It's Robert, really."

Starr, from his maturer viewpoint of the early forties, liked young Robert, who was twenty-two. He believed that he understood the youngster and felt worried and sorry for the desperate physical and moral wreckage that Robert was making of his life. Their professional contacts had been futile, for Robert would pleasantly agree to a course of treatment and then willfully refuse to follow it through. In fact, Starr had declined any longer to accept him as a patient and had advised a sanitarium, advice which had ended in nowhere. He continued, however, to golf with him occasionally, usually when Robert was recovering from a debauch.

Stories about Robert's gambling losses were common gossip at the country club, mainly from wonder as to where he got the money with which to pay his debts. His allowance from Arthur, who was sixteen years older, was notoriously meager. Arthur, at the sudden death of their parents in a motor accident in the French Alps, had inherited the entire Chanin estate, whereas Robert (he had early in life been the perfect problem child) had been cut off with a dollar and a thumping codicil of outraged censure.

"Another scrape?" Starr asked.

"A culmination of successive ones rather."

"Just how, Mrs. Chanin?"

The delicate lifting of her shoulders was a work of art.

"You see, this time there's a girl."

"But hasn't there frequently been?"

"Yes, but not like this. Robert married her last night."

"Did you know her?"

"No, no one knows her."

It was more than a simple statement of fact; it was an epitaph.

"Have you seen her, Mrs. Chanin?"

"Yes. Robert brought her here this morning. I liked her, Doctor. I hope that won't strike you as extraordinary."

"Why should it, Mrs. Chanin?"

"Well, there was a flavor; nothing definite was said about it, but one sensed the district."

"Oh, surely not!"

"Robert was very drunk, Doctor. The girl's name is Beatrice. She's sixteen. She's thin from something. I thought it hunger. It made her eyes seem very large, so that you ignored the rest of her. Robert introduced her—well, defiantly. To me and to Arthur. It wasn't pleasant."

"No, I can understand that."

"I wondered at his temerity in bringing her so abruptly, without any warning, to the house. But then you know the tragic fog that Robert lives in. Is it too much to suggest that he loves her? I mean to a point that blinded any shred of common sense? I prefer that to the other."

"Which other, Mrs. Chanin?"

"The more obvious interpretation, Doctor. Plain extortion, frankly. A drunken attempt to force Arthur to protect the Chanin name by an offer to annul the mésalliance in exchange for a lump sum. They stayed for lunch."

"What?"

Her smile was deprecatingly understanding and forgiving too.

"Do you know Arthur well?"

"Actually, I don't."

"So many people have what you might call their family side."

"Yes, I see what you mean."

"The fact that he asked them to stay for lunch was a case in point. That was when Arthur told them, you see. Possibly it's why I decided to like her, the way she bore up under Arthur's smiling insistence that Robert have second servings in honor of it being the Prodigal's last meal. They stood it until the salad course when Arthur—well, it would have been kinder to throw them out physically than the way in which Arthur did. That was when the district note was touched. And there you are. I thought you had better know in case you were puzzled by any nervous disorders beyond plain indigestion. Will you see me before you go?"

"Of course, Mrs. Chanin."

The house held a definite brooding quality as he mounted the stairs. He rapped lightly on the door of Arthur Chanin's bedroom. There was no answer. He went inside the vast, still room with its large front windows that overlooked the river. It retained the "modern taste" of the early

1880s when ebony veneers, straight lines and holly inlays had thrown the Mid-Victorian overboard.

A single lamp burned on a table beside the massive canopy bed, turning Arthur Chanin's face into a gray dish against white pillows. It was a weakly patrician face, sensual in a petulant way, topped by black hair cut with a Byronic touch. Starr thought him sleeping, but his eyes opened and he said, "I'm sick. I've just been very sick, in there, in the bathroom. Got cramps."

Starr glanced toward the open bathroom door. The lights in the bathroom were out, but his eye was caught for an instant by a lambent glow of pale moonlight that illumined some patch of moisture at the base of the wide marble washstand.

"Doctor—"

"Yes?"

(*No further response—temperature—surely an obvious case of acute gastroenteritis, augmented by nervous reaction to the luncheon scene—then, swiftly, a flash of delirium—the blank, bland eyes of sudden coma—cardiac collapse—*)

Starr did not know that Mrs. Chanin was beside him until he heard her voice. "Doctor?"

"Mrs. Chanin!"

"Arthur? Oh, dear God—Arthur—"

"Yes. He's dead."

"*Oh, darling—darling—darling—*"

The violence of her grief upset him. It was genuine enough. He did believe that. But there was something in its curious intensity that was frightening too.

* * * *

A clock struck half-past ten.

Dr. Starr put the fountain pen down on his desk. He looked up at his secretary as she stood, in severe white, in the office doorway.

"Yes, Miss Wadsworth?"

"Mr. Robert Chanin is here."

"Show him in, please."

"Yes, Doctor."

Starr shoved the blank death certificate further to one side. He stood up. He held out his hand as Robert Chanin came through the doorway.

"Sorry, Bob."

"Thanks, Colin."

"Drink?"

"Please."

Starr poured scotch.

"Sit down."

"Thanks."

Starr appraised shaky fingers, the rangy looseness of the youngster's body, the dull chalk of haunted shock under the homely, pleasant face's tan.

"There was nothing I could do, nothing anyone could do. Those things happen."

"Sure, Colin."

"Who told you?"

"Edna."

"She knew where you were?"

"Yes. Beatrice and I checked in at the Muskingum House this afternoon. Edna telephoned. She said I'd better run over and see you before going out to the house. She said there'd be things you'd want to know for the death certificate."

"That's right. More scotch?"

"No, thanks, Colin. Got too much now."

Starr jotted down notes.

"When was your brother born?"

"In 1901, July eleventh."

"Your father's full name?"

"Jackson Arthur Chanin."

"Also born in Laurel Falls?"

"Yes."

"Your mother's maiden name?"

"Ellen May Beston."

"Where born?"

"Here too."

The office door opened.

"Yes, Miss Wadsworth?"

"Mr. Greentree is on the wire, Doctor. He's telephoning directly from Mr. Chanin's home, not the funeral parlors."

"Thank you."

Starr lifted the phone from its cradle. He noted the increasing nervousness of Robert's fingers as the youngster took a match from his pocket and snapped it alight with a thumbnail, rather a large match, like the old-timers. "Greentree?"

"Oh, hello, Doc. I'm out at the Chanin place. Mrs. Chanin says a cremation, and, boy, is she splashing! You know that Number 74 casket? Solid silver handles and the imported violet crepe? Like the Whitmans fell for last November?"

"Yes…"

"Well, is it okay to go ahead, or do I wait until you fill out the certificate? Guess that's a laugh!"

Starr looked beyond the desk, beyond Robert Chanin, past the long old-timer match still burning in his fingers, out through a window at the silhouette of Lombardy poplars done in laced ebony against the black night sky—*against the black night sky*—a shock ran lightly along his nerves and grew with swift, illuminating impacts into a chill monstrosity that widened his eyes.

"Doc?" Greentree's voice over the telephone was querulous. "Are you still there, Doc?"

"Yes…"

"I asked was it all right to go ahead."

"What?"

"The death certificate, Doc. Have I got your say-so to go ahead?"

"Wait."

"Wait?"

"I'll be out there shortly."

"But what the hell, Doc? Going formal on me?"

"I said wait."

Starr put the phone back on its cradle. Chill prickles still iced his nerves. He took a cigarette. He said, "Got a match, Bob?"

"Sure."

Starr accepted the match. He fiddled with it. He did not light it. He said, "Look here, do you mind if I get pretty personal?"

"Go right ahead."

"Where did you get it?"

"Get what?"

"Money."

"You've been hearing things?"

"Plenty of things."

"I see."

"Don't get tough, mutt. I like you."

"I've always thought you did."

"Well?"

"Edna gave it to me. Sorry to disappoint the old cocktail bags at the club Sorry it wasn't armed holdups."

"Was it her own money?"

"Edna's got no money. She'd get it from Arthur, heaven knows how. It can't do her any harm now, no matter who knows it."

"She's been pretty decent to you?"

"Decent? She's an angel. I guess nobody'll ever know what she's been to me since she married Arthur. She understands me. Nothing, no matter what happened, Colin, she'd come right up to bat with money or sympathy. Honest, no matter what I did she'd just say it was all right and how she understood."

"Did it ever strike you that perhaps the sympathy could be—well, encouragement?"

Sweat broke on Robert's strained young face.

"Why, you dirty-minded louse, I—" He started to cry. "Honest to God, Colin, if I ever thought anything like that—"

Starr waited until Robert had finished crying. He stood up.

"Wait outside for me, please, Bob."

"All right, Colin."

The office door closed. Starr lifted the telephone. He made two calls. The first one took ten minutes. The second one longer.

He put the unlighted match in his pocket.

* * * *

Mrs. Chanin had changed into black.

The small drawing room seemed dimmer than before, the *putti* vaguer, a more misty pink; the scent of Mrs. Chanin's lethal perfume alone remained strong. "But surely Robert gave you the details, Doctor?"

"There are further ones I need for the diagnosis, Mrs. Chanin. What time was luncheon?"

"At one o'clock. No—do you want this quite exact?"

"Quite, please."

"Robert and his wife came shortly before, and Arthur started smiling and being courtly in the manner which he thought so amusing and insisted that they stay for lunch. Robert went upstairs to his room to pack some things and left the girl with us."

"How long was Robert gone?"

"About half an hour, I think. I know we delayed luncheon until Maxwell told us that Robert was already in the dining room mixing a scotch and soda."

"Was there any food on the table before you sat down?"

"The salad, Doctor—Arthur's one touch of provincialism. He liked it to be there at luncheon."

"Any garlic in it?"

"Yes, a trace. Maxwell rubs the bowl."

"What sort of a salad, Mrs. Chanin?"

"Nothing alarming, Doctor. I'm afraid you will have to attribute the enteritis to the nervous tension rather than the food."

"I would still like to know the contents of the salad."

He carefully noted her eyes as they shifted slightly to the doorway behind him.

"Greens, some lettuce and romaine, some radishes, stuffed olives—Arthur's own recipe, as a matter of fact. His thought on salads was to sublimate them."

"You did hate him, didn't you?"

"Yes." Blood flushed her cheeks slowly, then slowly drained, and they were white again. "Are you being deliberately impertinent?"

"Your husband was murdered, Mrs. Chanin."

She said after a long while, while her eyes continued to flick obliquely toward the door behind him, "When did you know?"

"You thought so too?"

"I was afraid." She started to tremble. "I am afraid." She leaned toward him, and her fingers were icy on his hand. "Poison, Doctor?"

He took the match which Robert had given him from his pocket.

"Have you ever noticed any matches of this type in the house?"

"It's rather large, isn't it? Weren't they more common in the gaslight era?"

"They were common before the law prevented their manufacture."

"Fire? Spontaneous combustion?"

"No, their heads contain the toxic form of phosphorus. The law now insists that a harmless, a nontoxic form be used instead."

"But, surely—just a match, Doctor?"

Starr studied her quietly while trying to hold back the increased pressure of his blood, while conscious of the light beading of sweat that was starting on his face.

"As little as one and one half grains has fatally poisoned an adult, Mrs. Chanin. You can check that, if it interests you, in the book on legal medicine and toxicology in your husband's library. There are cases on record where children have sucked the ends of lucifer matches and where the ends of just two of them have been known to kill a child. Were you aware of any matches such as this one in the house?"

The room, the night itself could not have been more still. No sign of her inward struggle touched the placid beauty of her face.

"Were you, Mrs. Chanin?"

"Yes, Doctor."

"Tell me, please."

"Are you familiar with those old-fashioned china figures which come apart?"

"No, Mrs. Chanin."

"Their base is a jar, and the top part lifts off and forms a lid. Robert found one of them in the attic. He brought it down and showed it to me. There were matches in it—that type of match, Doctor. He said there were enough to kill everyone in the house. Naturally, I accepted the reference as to fire."

"Robert took the matches?"

"He took the jar into his room. I imagine it is still there."

"Have you any idea how he would know of the poisonous nature of phosphorus?"

"Not specifically of phosphorus—"

"But poisons?"

"He has spoken of poisons. He was reading, only last week, that book on toxicology which you just referred to."

"Mrs. Chanin—"

"Doctor?"

"We both of us are faced with making a grave decision. I am satisfied that an autopsy will bear out my contention that your husband died from phosphorus poisoning. I suggest that several lucifer match heads were introduced into his portion of salad, because phosphorus has the taste and odor of garlic and because the consistency of the match heads would be comparable to the brittle consistency of a radish. Concerning my own decision, I have no alternative. I must instruct the coroner that an autopsy should be performed."

"And mine, Doctor?"

"Whether to accuse Robert of the crime or to confess to it yourself."

He had once in the hills seen an adder contract stiffly and then stay tensed while weighing the advantage of a lunge. Her slight laugh, when it came, did not dissolve the picture. Her eyes returned to the door.

"Are you seriously suggesting, Doctor, that after all I've done for that rotten, drunken, degenerate young fool—after I've made myself sick with having to shield Arthur from Robert's fool excesses—you speak of decisions? Yes, I'll accuse him—list his hatred of his brother—brand his motive as the hope that with Arthur dead he could get Arthur's money through my weakness, my forced sympathy—"

Abruptly, she was still.

Waiting.

The shot was muted by the ceiling and the heavy walls, but its identity was unmistakable.

Something like a sigh escaped her.

"It's better that way, Doctor. Robert was listening, you see. He was standing at the door."

He continued to sit there quietly, looking at her.

"Why don't you go to him?" she said sharply. "Perhaps you can save him!"

"Your influence over Robert was stronger than I thought. Don't you wan him to die, Mrs. Chanin, too?"

The tension was like the hush before thunder.

"You fool!" she said impulsively.

"No, Mrs. Chanin. I know how things are. I know how you purposely debauched him with money and encouragement until he idolized you and became a drunken slave in his adoration of you."

Her voice had the texture of glare ice.

"Why?"

"To make Robert the logical suspect if your husband's death should, by some fluke, be recognized as murder when you killed him."

"Why?"

"I don't know that swimming instructor's name, Mrs. Chanin, but I do know that his hair is blond and that your hair and Mr. Chanin's hair is black."

Her lips grew hard and tight and revealed her teeth unpleasantly. She struck him a vicious slap across the face.

"I called you a fool, Doctor, and you are one." Her voice rose to the exultant, ungovernable pitch of a paranoiac. "Robert's suicide is a confession of guilt. Nothing can touch me now; not you, not the law, not even God, Doctor."

"Thank you, Mrs. Chanin."

"What?"

"For having just confessed your guilt."

Her grimace became more sickening.

"Where are your witnesses, Doctor?"

Then, again, she looked toward the door. Flames burned hotly in her head as Robert came into the room and two men. She noticed absently that one of the men carried a notebook and a pencil. She heard someone talking and believed that it was Dr. Starr, saying, "I don't think you've met District Attorney Heffernan, Mrs. Chanin. And this is his stenographer, Aleck Jones."

* * * *

A clock struck four, and daybreak thinned the dark sky toward the east.

Miss Wadsworth placed the steaming cup of black coffee on the desk. He asked her to sit down. He told her of the difficulties involved in obtaining a conviction in homicides from poison unless the poisoner could be forced to confess. He told of his arrangement with the district attorney and with Robert in regard to the revolver shot. He asked her to make a note regarding a wedding present for Robert and his wife. He said that Robert was again under his care and that there would be excellent hope for a lasting cure, now that the law had removed the cancerous growth that had been killing his soul. He said that he was desperately tired and that she must be desperately tired and that both of them had better call it a day.

"There's just one thing, Doctor."

"Yes, Miss Wadsworth?"

"You were going to fill in the death certificate as an ordinary case of acute gastroenteritis just before Mr. Robert Chanin came here. Do you mind my asking what made you change your mind, what made you realize it was murder?"

"Moonlight."

"But there was no moon tonight, Doctor."

"I know. That's just the point."

He told her of the darkened bathroom seen through the open doorway of Arthur Chanin's room, of the lambent glow like pale moonlight that had illumined some patch of moisture at the base of the wide marble washstand, where Arthur had been violently ill, of the habit of such stomach matter to glow faintly in the dark in cases of phosphorus poisoning. He told her he had accepted it automatically as a reflection of the moon and had dismissed it from his mind until Greentree had been telephoning, then he had noticed through the window that the night was black and that there was no moon, and so, in connotation with the lucifer match that had still been burning in Robert's fingers—Yes, on the whole, it had verged on the perfect crime.

THE CASE OF THE
SUDDEN SHOT

The bullet was lead and had been activated by the comparatively low velocity of a revolver shot, comparative, that is, with one from an automatic or a machine gun or a rifle. But its job had been thorough.

Dr. Colin Starr listed it for his own satisfaction as a lung wound involving the perforation of a large trunk of the pulmonary vein, with profuse bleeding into the chest cavity and with death occurring within a few minutes. He felt that the coroner, when he came, would concur.

The bullet's caliber he placed at .38, a "short." Attached to it was what he believed would prove to be a splinter of rib, and he thought that the track would pass uneccentrically through the chest.

The tip of the bullet protruded from the exit hole.

He looked thoughtfully at the pattern and amount of blood which stained the immediate area where the body lay.

He said to Patrolman Brostrom, "Hunt up a reading glass, will you? Try the library. Ask a servant, if you have to, but don't disturb Mrs. Fraley." He saw the damp prelude to nausea on Brostrom's stolid face. "Take a shot of whisky or brandy before you come back."

"I certainly will, Doctor."

Brostrom left the living room. It was a pleasant room, set in the gracious tranquility of an earlier day and unchanged through four generations of Fraleys. Its French windows opened onto lawn and the moist, still air of a summer daybreak. Beyond the lawn lay the acres of the Fraley estate, walled off at their western end from the fairways of the country club's golf course and at the east by Ludington Road and the Muskingum River.

On the floor of the room was the body, naked except for a brief pair of swimming trunks, lanky with youth and topped by the lean, spiritual face of Dean Ludington. Eleven feet away from it, on the edge of an Aubusson carpet, was the revolver.

Starr looked at the thin perfection of the platinum wrist watch which Bob Chanin had insisted on giving him after he had solved, last June, the lucifer-match murder of Bob's brother. It was half-past four.

He took the pearl-handled magnifying glass from Patrolman Brostrom, who looked better, and asked Brostrom to move a reading lamp onto the floor beside the body.

Starr adjusted the lamp's shade so that light shafted young Ludington's brown torso. He confirmed his belief that the splinter adhering to the lead bullet was rib bone.

He turned his attention to the entrance wound and, with the delicate application of an instrument from his bag, collected some minute bits of cloth. He placed them on a prescription blank, folded the blank and put it in his pocket.

A siren wailed through the quiet of the night.

"That'll be the boys," Brostrom said.

* * * *

Starr's report to District Attorney Thomas Heffernan was brief. Aleck Jones, Heffernan's stenographer, took it down as they stood drinking steaming black coffee in the dining room.

He, Starr said, had been awakened by a telephone call from the Fraley home shortly before half-past three. Mrs. Chesterton Fraley was on the wire and had told him in a voice broken with hysteria that she had heard a shot. She had got out of bed and run downstairs and into the living room where the lights were on. She had found her young neighbor, Dean Ludington, on the floor dead. She had found her son, Jock Fraley, in the washroom that opened off the main hall being desperately, violently ill. Jock was beside her right then, while she telephoned, in a state of collapse.

Starr had dressed and come, the dressing taking ten minutes, the two-mile ride three. He had reached the Fraley's about ten of four.

Patrolman Brostrom, who covered Ludington Road on a motorcycle, was already there, having been interested in the untimely lights that burned in the Fraley house and in one shriek from a neurotic maid. Starr had found Mrs. Fraley and her son in the library. She had pulled herself together, but the anguish and worry stamped on her face made her look like death. Jock Fraley was a wreck both mentally and physically.

Jock Fraley had confessed to the crime.

"It's a rotten shame," Heffernan said, "letting kids go haywire like that. It's the parents' fault, I say, and still that boy has to take the rap for it. Maybe if his father were living things would be different. How old is he, anyhow, Colin?"

"He was twenty-two last May."

"What sort of shape is he in now?"

"He's better."

"What was he? Just blind drunk?"

"No, it wasn't entirely liquor. He'd been smoking marijuana."

"I've heard some of that filthy stuff was around."

"Jock didn't know he was smoking it. He doesn't know where he got the cigarettes."

"That doesn't make sense."

"I think it does, Tom. I think so because there are several things about Dean Ludington's death that make sense just as queerly. There's a bare chance Jock didn't do it."

"Listen, Colin, he said he did it. Did you get the idea he was covering for somebody?"

"No, that sort of heroic idiocy just doesn't happen. Jock thinks he did it all right, but here's the point, Tom: he doesn't know why."

"I get it. Accidental homicide while under the influence of liquor, or else a temporary-insanity plea."

"Jock just hasn't got that kind of a mind, and you know it."

"I know he's confessed. I also know a confession isn't worth a damn without corroborative evidence. Well, there's plenty."

"Feel like loosening up?"

"Sure, why not? I'm not trying to railroad the boy, but I've got to use common sense. You examined the body, so you know the wound must have been a contact one and that the body was naked except for swimming trunks."

"I took some of the bits of cloth from the entrance wound."

"So has the coroner, and so the gun was fired through cloth, through a coat pocket."

"There's no hole in any pocket of the tuxedo jacket Jock was wearing when I got here."

"I know that. But there's a bullet hole and a flame burn in the pocket of a tweed jacket of Jock's that was hanging in his clothes closet."

"You're arguing that he changed his coat just to shoot Dean Ludington?"

"Can you name me accurately any seven things a drunk will do when he's out on his feet?"

"No, I can't."

"All right. My bet is that microphotographs of the cloth bits that were taken from the wound will check with the cloth of the tweed jacket."

"And what was the motive?"

"Listen, Colin, people have got tight and shot other people dead for nothing more than a word or two so frequently that it's a headache. The police blotters of any town of any size crawl with it. Dean Ludington takes a dip in his swimming pool. We know that because his trunks are wet. He comes over here and starts jawing with Jock in the living room, and Jock shoots him. What they jawed about I'll find out when I put the screws on Jock."

"Let me take a crack at him first, will you? I yanked him through grippe last winter and I've glued him together every time he's fallen of his horse. He does it so frequently I suspect Windsor blood. He'll talk to me. Really talk."

"All right, go ahead." Heffernan stared at Starr sharply. "What's at the bottom of this? What's bothering you?"

"Take a good look at the blood pattern on that carpet," Starr said, "then tell me if it means what I think it does."

* * * *

Jock Fraley was lying on his bed. A white tuxedo jacket lay across the back of a chair. His shoes were oft. His plain, wholesome young face, topped by a shock of chestnut hair, looked better but not much. Mrs. Fraley had seen to his jacket and shoes. She sat beside the bed, in wool and marabou, a quiet frail woman with quiet hands and tortured deep gray eyes.

"Shall I leave, Doctor?"

"Would you mind, Mrs. Fraley?"

"Of course not."

"Feel any better, Jock?"

"Guess so, Colin."

"Figured any reason yet for shooting Dean?"

"I just remember the gun being in my hand when I came to. The sound of the shot must have snapped me out of it. I don't know how long I'd been out on my feet. Ever get that way, Colin?"

"Once, on absinthe, and only once."

"Fierce, isn't it?"

"Terrible. Your best friends all tell you the next day just what you did and just what you said. I know I blocked traffic for a while by sitting in front of a street car and making noises like a cow."

"Sure enough?"

"Yes. My medical-school days. Fortunately they preceded the current trend toward euthanasia or I wouldn't be here now, trying to get you out of this mess."

"Thanks, Colin, but I don't want any temporary-insanity-plea stuff. I want to take what's coming to me. Why wouldn't I? He was Elsa's brother, wasn't he?" The spoken sound of her name itself was enough to start him crying. "I want to die, Colin."

"All right. You will in time. What good will it do Elsa?"

"We got engaged last week."

This was news. Elsa Ludington was nineteen and one of the prettiest kids in town, as well as being in line to inherit one of the largest fortunes in the state. "You kept it pretty quiet," Starr said.

"Elsa wanted it that way until her folks got back. Nobody knows, only Phil."

"Which Phil?"

"Phil Taylor." Jock turned his face to the wall. "Phil was engaged to her secretly and she broke it off when she told him about me, about how she suddenly knew it had always been me only I'd been such a damn clam about it. Phil took it like a brick. How quick does it take, Colin? I mean counting the trial and everything?"

"I guess they can make it pretty fast if you ask them to. Listen, you young damn fool, you pulled a blank and some pretty queer things happened during it, until the sound of a sudden shot snapped you out of it. I'm going to fill that blank in. Blow your nose and get down to business."

"Huh!"

"Was it your revolver?"

"Yes. It's an old one that belonged to Dad."

"Where is it kept?"

"In the desk in the library."

"Who knows that?"

"Anybody in the crowd, I guess. We've used it plenty for target practice."

"Give me the exact setup for last evening."

"From when?"

"From when you started to get a bag on."

"That was at Spinelli's."

Spinelli's was the roadhouse currently in vogue among the men and women of the town's youngest set, the set's average age centering around a mature eighteen. It boasted the stickiest band in Ohio and should, Starr thought, be gently removed from the local scene with a few judicious sticks of dynamite.

"Who was there?"

"Everybody, Colin."

"That's fine. Suppose you break them down into small pieces?"

"But what's the use? Nothing but a miracle could change my having done it."

"All right, we'll look for a miracle. We'll also look for the rat who set the stage. And stop wasting time. Who was there?"

Starr's voice was strengthening, like the bracing feel of cold water when you plunge in, sweating, on a hot summer's day, and the tension loosened a little on Jock's face.

"Elsa was with me," he said, "and Dean had that new bolt of lightning who's staying with the Atchinsons along, and Frank and Polly Atchinson were with us, and Phil joined us too."

"Phil Taylor?"

"Yes. Eldridge Taylor and Mabel brought him, and Mabel started being resigned and going in for her usual that's-right-leave-me-sitting-here-alone line, and Phil got fed up with it and came over to our table. Eldridge was in one of his walking-delegate moods."

Starr took a moment to straighten it out. The Taylors were Jock's neighbors to the north just as the Ludington's were his neighbors to the south. Mabel Taylor was Eldridge's wife, and Phil was Eldridge's younger brother, younger by about twelve years. Starr knew the Taylors only casually. He had never treated them professionally, and their social scheme rarely extended beyond Laurel Falls' agreeable little group of sophisticates whose sport and relaxations were bounded by Gertrude Stein, gin and tonic and numerous cerebral forms of charades. He understood that Mabel was an adept at the harp, which had always stopped him right there.

He knew Eldridge Taylor as an enormously stout, platter-faced man with a great reputation for intellectual quips and a bright, detailed mind. He knew that Eldridge, as an architect, was reputed to be slipping and that he had recently lost out on several important local and state jobs.

He knew Philip Taylor as a leaner edition of his older brother, more along the lines of Jock's build, but otherwise he didn't know him at all.

"What time was all this, Jock?"

"We got to Spinelli's about half-past eleven. We'd been to the second show at the Bijou. You ought to go see it, Colin. Lugosi blows up the Gatun locks."

"Good. Were the Taylors at Spinelli's when you got there?"

"No they came in after."

"How long after?"

"A couple of dances, about half an hour, I guess."

"That takes us to midnight. Now about those marijuana cigarettes?"

"Honest, Colin, I swear I didn't know I was smoking that rotten stuff. I'd rather cut my hand off than do it, Colin."

"What kind were you smoking?"

"The same as I always do."

"Package or cigarette case?"

"Package."

"Full or nearly empty?"

"Say!"

"Yes?"

"That could be it, and she didn't want to be an old maid."

"Who didn't?"

"Lightning. And I could swear there were more than just one in the package when I left the table."

"I want this quite plain, Jock."

"It is. I know there were two or three in the package when we got up to dance."

"Did you keep the package on the table?"

"Yes, all of us did."

"Just who was at the table right then?"

"Like I said, Colin, Elsa and me, Dean and Miss Luffbart—she's Lightning—and Frank and Polly Atchison and Phil."

"Did you all get up to dance?"

"Yes."

"Phil Taylor was an odd man. What did he do?"

"He said he was going out to the bar for a quick one."

"Then you did leave Phil sitting at the table when the rest of you got up to dance?"

"Yes, to be technical about it."

"We've got to be technical. Go on."

"Well, the band quit playing and we sat down, and Dean ordered another round of rum slings for us men and ginger ale for the beetles."

"Was Phil Taylor there at the table when you got back?"

"No."

"Where was he?"

"I don't know."

"Get to the cigarette."

"Just as I said, Colin, I offered the pack to Miss Luffbart, and she said she didn't want to be an old maid because there was only one cigarette in it, so I lit it myself and ordered a fresh pack."

"That was the marijuana cigarette. There are two more in your coat pocket."

"There are?"

"Yes. Didn't it taste funny to you?"

"After six rum slings, Colin? Gosh, you could feed me corn silk."

"That's right. What time was it then?"

"A little after one, I think."

"What's the last thing you remember?"

"Dean getting up, I guess, to go over to the Taylor's table."

"Why?"

"I don't know why. Eldridge Taylor beckoned to him, I know, because Polly Atchinson said: Royal summons, Dean, don't forget the six steps backward before you turn when you leave, and Miss Luffbart told him to straighten his plumes, and about then is when I drew a blank and came to with the gun in my hand and, oh God, Colin, Dean was dead."

Starr leaped. He gripped Jock's wrist. He forced the razor blade from between his fingers. He landed a beauty precisely on Jock's button, then lifted the limp body onto the bed. He took a hypodermic syringe and shot an injection into Jock's arm. He opened the hall door and said to Mrs. Fraley, who was sitting close to it, as he knew she would be sitting close to it, "I've given Jock a sedative. Stay with him, Mrs. Fraley. And don't worry."

The Taylors had come across lawns: Eldridge and his wife Mabel and his younger brother Phil. The sirens had wakened them, and they had seen the Fraley lights. They had come over to find out what the trouble was and, if they could, to help. Starr saw them through the library doorway, being intellectually tense with Heffernan.

Starr said to Patrolman Brostrom, who was stolidly doing absolutely nothing in a hall chair, "Ask the district attorney to come here for a minute, please. Tell him the chief wants to see him."

"But he don't, Doctor. The chief's in the living room with the deceased."

"I know he don't, Brostrom. I do."

"Oh, I get it, Doctor. Leave it to me."

Starr led Heffernan into the dining room. He kept his voice low.

"Are you willing to stick out your neck?"

"What for, Colin?"

"To get a confession within the next hour."

"I'd be willing to become a giraffe. What's on your mind?"

"Housebreaking."

"What?"

Starr talked quietly, earnestly for several minutes. A queer sort of look settled slowly on District Attorney Heffernan's face.

"But that's crazy, Colin."

"Clinically, I think you're right."

* * * *

Starr joined the Taylors in the library. He thought absently that a harp was the perfect complement to Mabel Taylor's Rosetti glaze. She was a willowy woman, swathed in a dark velvet wrap over yards of clinging chiffon, and he suspected a supply of assorted neuroses that could be loosed at the drop of a hat.

The rum slings of Spinelli's were stamped in the gray and sweat of young Phil Taylor's face, giving its normally not unpleasant features a thinly saturnine effect, as if old age had suddenly moved in. Starr noticed that the tips of his fingers were club-shaped and that he was gripping them together in an effort to control their trembling.

Eldridge Taylor, from sheer bulk alone, dominated the scene. He attuned his voice to the accepted pitch for a house where high tragedy reigned.

He said, "I have just been talking to Heffernan, Doctor. I told him I might have known that Dean Ludington would come over here."

"Why, Mr. Taylor?"

"Because I know the smell of that stuff."

"Marijuana?"

"Yes. Muggles. One of my assistants in the office used to hit it. I caught him offering one to Phil."

"I didn't take it," Phil said truculently. "I knew what the damn stuff was."

"Naturally, Doctor, I gave the man the boot as soon as I found out, and I mean the boot." Eldridge's plate-shaped face slipped into a quiet smile. "Learned the trick up in the lumber country."

"What made you realize Jock was smoking it, Mr. Taylor?"

"I told you I smelled it."

"From your table?"

"Certainly not. The odor isn't as definite as that. I smelled it as I passed their table. I called Dean over and told him about it. Pitiful."

"Pitiful?"

"Well, isn't it? I think that's the charitable word. A young chap like Jock being a dope fiend and probably spreading the habit around among those kids."

"I'm beginning to see."

"I thought you would, Doctor. Dean probably didn't want to break it to Elsa until he'd thought it over. When he got home he couldn't sleep so he put on his trunks and took a dip in the swimming pool."

"Do you remember what time they left Spinelli's?"

"About one-thirty. Mabel and I left right afterward, after we'd resurrected Phil from a crap game with the bouncer."

"What condition would you say Jock was in, or didn't you notice?"

"I notice everything, Doctor. Jock was moving, talking over-exhilarated, naturally, but utterly unconscious of what he was doing. A walking blank. When he got to the parking lot we saw him drive off in his car alone. My reconstruction is this, Doctor: Dean, after his dip, decided to come over and have it out with Jock. Unquestionably he told Jock that the engagement to Elsa must be broken off. So Jock shot him. I repeat, pitiful!"

"A little too pat, Mr. Taylor."

"Pat? Of course it's pat. Life is pat. I dare say the most that Jock will get will be ten or twenty years. Heffernan agrees with me on the entire setup. Intelligent man, Heffernan; not at all like the ordinary politician. I shall testify for Jock at the trial, of course, as to the extenuating circumstances of his having been out on his feet."

"Mr. Heffernan did agree with you, Mr. Taylor."

"Did?"

"Yes."

A thick, still tension gripped the three Taylors. Chiffon rippled as Mabel stirred slightly in her chair. She said, "He doesn't now, Doctor?"

"No, Mrs. Taylor. The nature of Dean Ludington's wound indicates that he died within a minute or two and certainly retained no powers of locomotion."

"I fail to see the point, Doctor. Is it thought that he moved about the living room? It's most obscure."

"He wasn't killed in the living room."

The tension thickened, became, almost, a tangible thing.

"Really? Where was he killed, Doctor?"

"Beside the swimming pool on his own grounds, Mrs. Taylor."

Starr studied the bland, plate face of Eldridge Taylor; the gripped, club fingers of Phil; the tepid glint of something like fear that came into Mabel's violet-shadowed eyes.

"Conjecture, Doctor?" Eldridge Taylor said.

"No, a question of moisture and the lack of it."

"This is all very strange."

"Not really. Dean's swimming trunks were wet. He was killed beside the swimming pool, which is roughly two or three hundred yards across grounds from the living room of this house where his body was found. His body was either brought here in a car or was carried here across a man's shoulders. The only car when I got here was Jock's coupe, which is still parked in the driveway. If Jock had shot Dean at the swimming pool and then brought his body here in the car, for some fantastically inconceivable reason, there would be a wet patch on the cloth seat of Jock's car. There is none."

Mabel Taylor said softly, "So he carried him, then, Doctor?"

"If he had, Mrs. Taylor, there would be wet places either on Jock's white dinner jacket or on the tweed coat he was supposed to have been wearing when the shot was fired. There are none, and cloth dries very slowly in the humidity of a night like tonight."

"Tweed coat, Doctor?"

"A further elaboration to fasten the crime on Jock, Mrs. Taylor. As the coat isn't wet I believe that the killer did not wear it but fired through its pocket both to implicate Jock and to muffle the shot. Somewhere there is a car, Mrs. Taylor, with a damp patch on its seat, or there is a coat that not only has damp spots but, conceivably, blood spots as well."

Phil Taylor's voice was no longer truculent; it was thin and hard. "If Dean was killed beside his swimming pool how about that shot which wakened Mrs. Fraley? Which she heard from downstairs?"

"The killer fired that with his own gun. He fired it after he had placed Jock's gun, with which he had first shot Dean at the pool, in Jock's hand. The scene was an over-elaborate stage setting, yes, but it was devised by an over-elaborate mind. The definite purpose of that sudden shot, which wakened Mrs. Fraley and brought Jock to, was to raise the curtain on his play."

The door opened suddenly, almost as if on cue, and Patrolman Brostrom said rapidly, "Mrs. Fraley, Doctor—she's just taken something—the D. A. thinks it's iodine—"

Starr ran from the room. He whispered swiftly to Brostrom, "Nice job, Barrymore—beat it upstairs." He ran back along the hall and joined Heffernan on the back porch.

"It wasn't the car," Heffernan said. "It's hanging in the cupboard."

They sprinted across grass.

* * * *

The cupboard was roomy and racked with a row of suits. Starr stood with Heffernan in its darkness, getting his breath, hearing Heffernan getting his breath. They had not long to wait.

The door opened quietly onto paler darkness and a top light was snapped on, and a hand fumbled among suits.

"Is it this coat you're looking for?" Starr asked.

Eldridge Taylor's pale face quivered childishly. Then he screamed.

The mopping up wasn't nice. Diseases of the mind affronted Starr always, even though he understood them very well. The slipping of Taylor's business onto the shoals of ruin, the bright last hope of recouping through the marriage of his younger brother into the Ludington estate, its bitter dashing from his lips through the broken engagement and the ascendency of Jock, the diseased attempt to reverse by murder and a legal execution the scene again—one thing alone Taylor wanted to know: which facet of his inspired and opportune plan had betrayed him—how did Starr know that Ludington had not died where his body was found?

There was, Starr said, the blood, the excess of blood which stained the carpet where the body had been placed. And Taylor, screaming still, insisted that it was human blood, to which Starr agreed and said it didn't matter whether it were human blood or animal blood or plain red ink; its false message would have been the same.

He indicated the slight outline of a bandage beneath the trouser leg that hugged Taylor's large, plump calf, and Taylor screamed, Yes, it *was* his blood, which he had shed on the carpet in his fervor to set the stage with an accuracy that would defy suspicion! for, he insisted, where a shot man lay there must be blood.

In nine cases out of ten, Starr said, that would be true. But this had been the tenth. Apart from the fact that the bullet itself plugged up the wound of exit the bleeding with that type of injury was, with the exception of a drop or two, internal. So there should have been no blood.

"You'd better let me disinfect that cut on your calf, Mr. Taylor."

Taylor stared at him for a long moment, while a graying fear puckered his lips and etched sickening lines in his smooth round face as he viewed, in increasing clarity, that near and veiled horizon beyond which nothing lay.

"Does," he said, "it matter? Now?"

Starr felt small pity in his heart.

"I'm afraid it doesn't, Mr. Taylor. Not in the long run."

THE CASE OF THE
IMPERIOUS INVALID

The Marshalls' soiree musicale ended at eleven-thirty with Ross Fothergill's celebrated and interminable rendition of "Pale hands that gleam…" his own hands fluttering plumply from overshot cuffs, and the old house murmured with good-bys.

Dr. Colin Starr gave Janice Everett and Ludlow Dune a lift, Miss Everett to the estate next door where she wanted him to take a look at her sister Laura, after which he planned to drop Dune off on the way home.

Janice Everett sang, her acceptable contralto being one of Laurel Falls's happier exhibits, and it was inevitably turned on for any visitors of social or artistic note. She had at thirty-five the developed framework of a singer: a classical, dark-coroneted head poised regally over a decided bosom which tapered, with few indentations to speak about, to slender ankles and pretty little feet. Her fame remained local even though minor maestros who had sleeper-jumped into town through the years had flatteringly told her that it might easily become national in scope, while the latest one, in a haze of pates and champagne, had mellowly hinted at an ultimate haven in the Met.

Ludlow Dune, through those same years, had been her accompanist and coach; a largish forty, with swimming deep brown eyes and thick soft hair that rippled in a problematically natural curl. Whatever it was it did the trick and raised the hell up among the town's matrons who had turned the middle stretch.

As he stopped before the tall-columned porch Starr saw a glare of headlights in his rear-view mirror. A car swung alongside and braked, and Mary Everett jumped out and thanked the young Rallstons for a lovely evening and said good-by to young Roger Bennett in that caught, breathless sort, of voice with which, filled with wonder, she had been saying good-bys to Roger Bennett since spring. There were several hellos and more good-byes, and the Rallston kids and young Bennett swirled off in a hiss of crushed gravel.

It was, right then, a quarter to twelve.

Starr had thought frequently of Mary Bennett since she had come last spring to make her home with her cousins, the Misses Everett. She was a sweet, quiet youngster with a body that could stand fattening and a heart that needed (to replace her parents' sudden death) a lot of love. Starr doubted whether she had got it in the quantities required beneath the Everetts' solemn and massive gray slate roof. He was familiar with the home's ménage, having treated the elder Everett sister, Laura, for a persistent anemia during the past year.

There were, he knew, no servants beyond an outside handy man and a stolid Slavic woman who browsed through a general cleaning once a week and appeared in black alpaca and an unbecoming white cap at such rare evenings when the Everetts entertained.

Their roots struck back into the territorial period of Ohio. An Everett had notched his measure of Indians near the rapids of the Maumee during the battle of Fallen Timbers in 1794, when the Indians had lain in ambush behind tree trunks felled by storm. The sisters' grandfather had been a member of the Democratic Congressional delegation which had been hatched from dissatisfaction with the President's emancipation program in 1862. The sisters' father ("dear Papa") had manufactured, in addition to a comfortable fortune, shoes. He had died, leaving Laura and Janice jointly the estate, with Laura as trustee for Janice's share of it until Janice became twenty-five. And it had shrunk through two depressions to a husk in which Janice practiced liquid scales and Laura, with appropriate and expensive delicacies, enjoyed the semi-invalid trappings of her anemia.

Starr suspected strongly that Mary had done the bulk of the work since her arrival in spring, feeding on simple things (the tidbits being segregated carefully for poor Laura) and, more fulsomely, on her obvious love for young Roger Bennett. For whenever, rarely, Starr saw them together it was an obvious thing. He thought it pretty hopeless, too, unless they were willing to wait until Bennett's job in a filling station could economically reach even the cottage stage.

The hour was thirteen of twelve when Starr, Dune, Mary and Janice Everett gathered on the porch, while Janice Everett took a key from her bag and unlocked the front door. They went inside, into a large hallway dimly lighted by a ceiling cluster, and Janice Everett swept them along in her wake into a living room and said, "Scotch, Doctor? I know you do, Ludlow. Mary, my dear, you may light the fire."

It was chill and dampish in the room, with a musty smell that sifted from its faded elegance. Mary struck matches at the hearth, and Janice Everett dropped a black velvet wrap from her shoulders and blazed in crimson chiffon that had held their eye at the Marshalls' throughout a buffet supper at seven o'clock and the long musical evening. She handed the wrap to Dune, flashed her exit smile and left the room. Starr helped Mary at the hearth while Dune started harrying Debussy at the grand piano, and six minutes later they heard the scream.

It rang with startling precision and volume through the house, rooting them: Dune in a discord at the piano, Mary and Starr at the fire, and then Janice Everett was coming in from the hallway and saying, "Doctor—quickly, please, Doctor—Laura has killed herself."

Starr took the silver tray from her hands, with its three filled glasses of scotch and soda and ice, and put it on a table. She still held the doorway, a bulk of crimson chiffon and wide terrified eyes. She said, as he hurried past her, "Gas—gas!"

* * * *

The bedroom was on the ground floor. Laura Everett had not cared, with her anemia, to bother with stairs so she had converted a small parlor to her use and had transformed an adjoining coatroom into a bathroom.

Starr turned off the gas. Its source was obvious from the rubber tubing which led from beneath the towel covering Laura Everett's face to a baseboard outlet planned to supply fuel for a portable hot-water radiator beside the bed. He unbolted windows, opened them, then assured himself that Miss Everett was dead and had been dead, he judged superficially, for about three hours.

(Lividity well developed—suggillations, the settling through gravity of stagnant blood, were plain—the flesh cold, its lividities a dullish blue—a dullish blue—)

Starr went over to the hall door where Dune stood wiping dampness from an ashen face.

"There's nothing I can do," Starr said. "She's been dead for several hours. Phone District Attorney Heffernan, please. He'll know whom to call up and bring out here."

"Police?"

"Police, the coroner, Heffernan will see to it."

"But surely with a plain suicide, Doctor?"

"A suicide is governed by the regulations of any unnatural death. After you telephone stay in the living room with the Everetts."

"Of course, Doctor—yes, of course."

Starr closed the door. He returned to the bed. The room was remarkably clear of gas. His examination became more detailed and complete. He confirmed with greater accuracy, through body temperature, his guess that Miss Everett had been dead for about three hours: since, roughly, nine o'clock.

He looked for the inevitable suicide note.

There was none that he could see. Its absence puzzled him. He knew that a person under stress of strong emotion inevitably reacted to established patterns. Rarely had his experience shown him an exception, and definitely (he thought) there should be none now. Nothing in life was so cataclysmic as the moment of death, effacing all resources of initiative, compelling the mind in its bewilderment to snatch at and cling to accepted gestures which were known, again and again, to have been done. Whether one died (Starr knew this to be true) or whether one killed.

A book lay open on the bed table. A pencil was beside it, and black lead underlined heavily certain words on the open pages of the book. The book was Septimus Strange's *Moon Madness in Tahiti*. The underlined words, when read consecutively, made sense. They read: "—forgive—but—life is a—torment—tired—better—this—"

So (Starr's virile, pleasant face grew grim): the inevitable suicide note.

* * * *

Starr went through the ground floor of the house, thoroughly testing each window and each door that led outside. Each was securely bolted or locked. He searched, more perfunctorily, the cellar, the upper story and the attic, moving quickly through the dank dark house which was large enough for a home and children and for children's children and which had become a decaying mockery for three and was now a tomb.

He returned to the living room, where the fire was a futile gesture on its hearth. The looks that greeted him were easy to assort, simple for his intimate knowledge of men and women, a knowledge which ran the emotional gamut of the human nerves and brain and heart and sometimes, in its ugliness or beauty, of the soul.

Dune's swimming eyes were tightened into something smug, some discount of an immediate future of which he already had a foretaste. Janice Everett's had acquired, Starr thought, a certain depth: a curious quality of perception as if she were increasingly aware of things to which she had been blind. Mary's alone were bruised by shock and grief and with that astounding incredulity of the vital young toward sudden death.

"You telephoned, Mr. Dune?" Starr said.

"Yes." Dune examined a large gold watch attached to a heavy-linked gold chain which thwarted his mid section over white piqué. "Ten after midnight. Any time now."

Janice Everett's voice was obviously controlled.

"Doctor—"

"Miss Everett?"

"Laura—surely she wasn't ill enough for that?"

"No, in no sense ill enough."

"Then why?" Suddenly she was shrill. "*Why?*"

"Janice, my sweet, my dear!"

Dune caught and stroked a hand which, becoming aware of the stroking after two or three of them, she jerked away. Blood drained from her cheeks, bringing out the old lines, and she said, before she collapsed, "Laura made her life exactly what it was, so I suppose she felt she had the right. The right to take it, Doctor."

Starr got a glass from the highballs which were still untouched upon the tray. He insisted that she drink some, watched color's slow return; then she wanted to be alone, to relieve by some solitary solace the feeling of suffocation that was stifling her (she said), so if they would forgive her going upstairs to her room for a little while, with her suffocation and her grief—no, not Mary or Dune, just alone.

Her departure was Wagnerian. It left a void for them to rattle in. There were things Starr wanted to know. He said to Mary, "About tonight, was the maid here?"

"No, Doctor, Anna's day is Friday."

"Miss Everett was alone?"

"Yes, after Cousin Janice left and I left."

"When was that, Mary?"

"Cousin Janice left just before seven for the Marshalls'; then after Cousin Laura had finished her supper I took care of the dishes and filled the thermos jug with ice cubes, and Roger called for me with the Rallstons at eight."

"Had Miss Everett gone to bed?"

"She had supper in bed, Doctor. It was one of her bad days. I did want to stay home with her, but Cousin Janice said it was nonsense and insisted that I go to the party, but it wasn't nonsense; it wasn't all right."

Dune said sharply, "Why not? You can't foresee things like this. Perhaps I seem callous, but I've a philosophy about life. What's done is done."

"About the doors and windows, Mary?"

"Yes, Doctor?"

"Were they locked when you left?"

"Oh yes. I saw to that."

"You have a key?"

"I used Cousin Laura's."

"Who else has a key?"

"Only Cousin Janice."

"What's this all about?" Dune asked.

"The only gauge for a suicide, Mr. Dune, are the circumstances surrounding a case. They will be required in my report."

"Gauge? It seems perfectly plain. Two keys, one with Mary at the Rallstons', and Janice had the other one with us at the Marshalls', and Laura was locked up alone in the house. Isn't it?"

"Tell me about the party, Mary."

"We were on the river, Doctor, in Jerry Rallston's launch. Esther and Norman Towne met us at the boathouse and came with us. Esther and Jerry, well, I think they like each other the way Roger and I do. They're awfully good friends, I mean."

"Of course. Incidentally, I don't think I've seen much of you and Roger around, or does the awfully good friendship consist in telepathy? Or isn't it any of my business anyhow?"

Mary smiled back at him faintly.

"You know how things are, and then Cousin Laura—it was so silly, really."

"What was?"

"Well, just because Roger works in a filling station. His family's an awful good one, and all the crowd understands and admires him for it."

"But Miss Laura Everett didn't?"

"No. It isn't that she ever said anything directly, but it did seem hard ever to be able to keep a date with Roger. Things just came up."

"Did she try to keep your home tonight?"

"I think she wanted to, but I think Cousin Janice talked to her. I think Cousin Janice likes Roger a lot better than Cousin Laura did, or else she just doesn't mind his working in a filling station so much."

"I suppose you're right. Look here, you spoke of doing the dishes before you left and also of filling a thermos jug with ice cubes. Were they for your Cousin Laura?"

"No, they were for you. Cousin Janice said she was going to ask you to stop in on the way home, you and Mr. Dune, and she wanted the tray ready. She wanted you to see—Cousin Laura—"

She turned her face away in tears. Dune cleared his throat awkwardly, said: There, there! and a pull bell jangled in the hallway.

"That will be District Attorney Heffernan," Starr said.

* * * *

It was twenty after midnight.

Starr stood beside the bed with Heffernan in the cold, quiet room while Aleck Jones, Heffernan's stenographer, jotted down a preliminary report. Obviously (Heffernan insisted) a plain, straightforward case of suicide: an ill, a despondent woman securely locked from intruders in an empty house, no marks of violence, no signs of struggle in the bed or in the room, the suicide message in the book; why under the sun (Heffernan asked) had Starr sent for him? Why not just some assistant from the coroner's office to rubber-stamp an obvious case?

"It's obvious enough," Starr said. "But it's murder."

"Look here, Colin. Be reasonable. Take your time elements."

"I have."

"All right. Laura Everett was alive when Mary left her around eight o'clock. Or have you got some nutty idea that that nice kid killed her?"

"No, the facts wouldn't fit. She couldn't have."

"All right again. You and Dune and Mary and Janice Everett all come in together about midnight and find—this is your own say-so, mind you—you find that Laura Everett has been dead for three hours or since nine o'clock. So if Mary didn't do it before she left the house what's your only other answer? Some tramp who drifted in through locked doors and windows killed her without leaving any sign of a struggle, without robbery or any trace of a sane motive, and then drifted out again? Forgive the sarcasm if it seems pretty heavy, but honestly!"

"No tramp. I know who killed her."

"Shall we go around again? Mary? If that child's a murderess I'm one. Look at her. Look at me."

Starr did not smile. He said, "You might kill tonight."

"Rot."

"Y'might. Jones, here, might."

"Nonsense, Colin. We're three normal people."

"Normal? Yes, in the sense that you're romantic. We all are. We're that way as a nation. We accept all of the nicer clichés about life. In spite of rational fact we prefer womanhood on a pedestal, tender, soft, fine; you know that. Just look at your acquittals, look at the jury-trial balance between evidence and a pretty face. No, don't misunderstand me—I'll admit the infinite capacity of women for the finest standards we know, but I refuse to blind myself to the truth, that women can be inhumanly vicious, incredibly cruel. Like men. Given a common set of circumstances, no two individuals will react the same. Angels can become devils in the flash of an eye and the reverse. I know that, Tom."

Heffernan's jaw grew obstinate.

"That kid has more than a pretty face. She's got a good face. I'd go to bat on it. And in my job I know faces."

"There is no face to murder. It's unpredictable. It's a force as capricious as lightning." Starr gestured impatiently. "Take a hundred people at random. You can fairly pick out your liars, your thieves, your defectives and your cheats; yes, I'll grant you that. Any psychiatrist could do so with the simplicity of adding two to two and getting four. But to pick your murderers from that group? You can't. The psychiatrist can't. Nor can you pick any of the myriad potent or inconsequential motives which impel them to the kill."

"Listen, Colin. I know you're different from the rest of us, not just seeing things as a doctor which we miss, but in other ways too. You've put the bite on some tricky messes in this town, but facts don't lie. And right now they spell suicide in ABCs."

"Let me prove you're wrong. Get Jones to take down accurate notes on the condition of this body. Observe the things I'm going to point out to you, and be prepared to swear to them in court."

"What things?"

"Come closer—you, too, Jones. First, the lividity."

"What's lividity?"

"This"

* * * *

Brief solitude had had its quieting effect.

Janice Everett had a cold compress across her eyes. She lay vivid in crimson chiffon on a chaise-longue of faded lemon French corduroy and did not stir when Starr closed the room's hall door.

"Is it you, Doctor?"

"Yes, Miss Everett."

The room was spacious, with doors opening into a bedroom and a bathroom. Its earlier smartness had a mended look, and dust filmed flat surfaces of veneers. Starr drew a chair closer to the chaise-longue and sat down on threadbare brocade. He said nothing, and the silence grew, and the little noises of the house and the night became important out of all proportion to their sound.

Then: "Well, Doctor?"

"I've yet to express my sympathy, Miss Everett."

"Thank you. Docs one suffer—from asphyxia?"

"Briefly."

"Briefly, Doctor?"

He studied her white, quiet hands.

"Exact observation on the point has naturally been rare, Miss Everett."

"Naturally."

"However, there were some experiments conducted a good many years ago in England. They serve as a yardstick. This doesn't disturb you, Miss Everett?"

"Why? I mean if release from living meant happiness to Laura have we the right to judge? Even to grieve? What were the experiments, Doctor?"

"They were made by a committee of the English Medico-Chirurgical Society. From the nine tests on animals they found that the average duration of breathing, after any air source had been cut off, was four minutes and five seconds."

"But gas, Doctor. Surely gas would be quicker?"

"Gas, Miss Everett?"

A white hand tensed in a minute contraction. Still she did not remove the cold compress from her eyes.

"Surely? Gas?"

"There is a property about gas poisoning which I found absent from your sister. There should have been a fresh color to her face, a lifelike tint to her lips. I found, instead, lividities that were dull and blue."

"I simply don't understand, Doctor."

"Your sister died from suffocation."

"Forgive me if I seem obtuse, if I miss the importance of what you're driving at. Was it the towel across her face and not the gas that killed her?"

"Your sister was already dead, Miss Everett, before the gas was turned on." Her hands clenched briefly, then were quiet again.

"I am not a stupid woman, Doctor. I see where your thoughts are leading. I refuse to accept them even against fact."

"You are thinking of Mary, Miss Everett?"

"I am drawing the only conclusion that I can from what you say, and in face of every medical technicality I know firmly in my heart that you are wrong. You sent for the police, Doctor. Do they think as you think?"

"Yes."

"But what motive, what reason? There is none."

"District Attorney Heffernan would disagree. Surely you know the town's propensity for gossip, Miss Everett. The Leffton people's offer has been thoroughly discussed, their efforts to persuade your sister and you to sell this estate to further their subdivision plan for a group of cottages on small lots."

"What conceivable motive could that offer to Mary? If she were to have lulled us both, then, true, she is our closest relative and heir, or has Mr. Heffernan touched on the fantasy that that dear child has reserved my murder for some later date?"

"I'm simply pointing out the obvious, Miss Everett. Surely you'll agree that your sister was adamant in her refusal to consider the Leffton offer?"

"Doctor, did you know Laura? Know her really well?"

"Yes, I think very well."

Laura was, in his thoughts, alive again before him: a woman who possessed in its fullest measure the tyrannical strength of the conscious weak. They traded, these iron weaklings, on the ultimate sympathy of those who were bound to them by the ties of any close relationship. They traded on that innate repugnance of a kin to hurt, in little things, a being whom the sheer habit of years had accustomed you to love. In little things, which he knew had a fashion for cohering until they solidified with time into a solid big.

"She was considerably older than you. Miss Everett?"

"Yes, eleven years. A handicap which she never released, Doctor. An authority, a mother complex, I suppose."

"And you? Forgive me if I harp on this Leffton matter. Without your sister's—well, domination, would you have sold?"

"With a chance at last? Does anyone relish chains?"

Starr felt against his will a certain pity, a pity which sprang from his helpless inability in any problem of human behavior not to see and understand the other side. Heffernan, a judge, a jury might dismiss as tenuous the motive for her crime, so he recognized the imperative necessity for a confession which, buttressed by evidence of the clearest nature, would stand in court.

He himself found nothing tenuous in the reason for this killing which the average layman would segregate into the tabulation reserved for crimes against nature. The happenstance that Laura was her sister could even have enhanced her purpose rather than have deterred her from the act.

He saw the profile of her life from childhood: being told as a little girl what and what not to do by another, an authoritative girl eleven years her senior; then the stretch of years when Laura had acted as trustee for her, Janice's, share of the estate; it took no Freud to label the result of that ingrained habit of dependence, of deferring ever to Laura's judgment, to her command through those formative years. And it took time, Starr knew, to shake such a domination off, time and a strength of will power which Janice Everett did not possess.

Until finally all of the little things had cohered under the Leffton company's offer to hand over a moderate fortune in cash for the estate. It had not meant a moderate fortune to Janice Everett but, as she had just herself said, a release from chains: money in hand with which to set out (undoubtedly with Dune in tow) and enslave the world with her voice. Before it was too late.

Starr knew that therein lay the actual spark which had flashed the accumulative powder train to murder, knew how nothing on earth could be more maddening than the irresponsibility of a reasonless check made by a person in power, saw that damnable stubbornness of Laura's with the insensate flare of rage in which Janice Everett must have seen it: for Laura would not sell. Nor could she force Laura to sell. But under that unpredictable and horrendous blast when murder tempts as a sole release against a capriciously unfair impasse she could, and had, forced Laura to quit being alive.

Starr did not like the job he had to do.

"Did you lie upon your sister?" he asked quietly. "Press her face down in the pillows?"

He did not like the thought of Heffernan and of Jones with his notebook and pencil waiting like twin fates behind the bedroom's slightly opened door. But, more strongly than any of those things, he disliked a murder done by one you trust. He arranged his lancets coldly in his mind while the little noises of the house and of the night were prominent again, while blood receded from Janice's face and she took the compress from her eyes, and he saw them hard and pitiless as black glass.

"Did I understand you, Doctor?"

He said reasonably, "I think you found your sister resting on her side and that you simply turned her face downward, when you lay upon her, and pressed her face into the pillows."

He watched the profound reserves of hidden strength she drew upon, plugging the shock of fear before it reached her glass-hard eyes, tightening the slight preliminary quiver of her lips.

"Before leaving for the Marshalls'? Have you gone mad, Doctor? Must I remind you that Mary can prove that Laura was alive, that even while I was sitting beside you at supper Laura was alive?"

"Your sister was killed shortly before nine o'clock, Miss Everett. Just before you sang."

Her voice was beautifully freighted with derision.

"By me?"

"You're a clever woman, Miss Everett. I think all of the Marshalls' guests would swear that your crimson dress was constantly vivid in the general scene, with the exception of those few minutes just before you sang."

"While I sprayed my throat, Doctor?"

"While you were, presumably, spraying your throat in the little dressing room opening from the music room."

"I see." (Derision remained, but he found in her eyes, which were turned directly on him, the flat and deadly contemplation of a patient snake.) "I sprayed my throat. I left the dressing room by its garden door. I came home. I smothered Laura. I arranged the suicide scene, the tubing, the towel, the—"

Her voice dropped abruptly as a stone into the quiet pool of the night.

"The book, Miss Everett?"

"Book, Doctor?"

"With its underlined suicide message?"

"There was one?"

"Yes. Yours, Miss Everett. The only property for the scene which you had prepared in advance and which will prove premeditation, your intent to kill."

She smiled obscurely at some inner comfort.

"You are yourself my alibi for your absurdities, Doctor."

"I realized that. I did not, I do not feel flattered. You were with me during supper and later while we gathered in the music room. You were scheduled to sing at nine o'clock. It was exactly ten minutes to nine when you asked me the time."

The strange smile lingered.

"And I sang, I think, as the clock struck the hour?"

"Yes, Miss Everett."

"So in ten minutes I did all of those things?"

"No, what you did was this. At ten minutes of nine you left me and went to the dressing room, bolting its music-room door. You did not spray your throat. You left by the garden door. You ran through the Marshalls' garden, across your own lawn, unlocked the front door and entered this house. We tested the time required to do so just before I came upstairs. It can be done in two minutes. You went directly to your sister's bedroom. You smothered her."

"Four minutes and five seconds, the average time it takes, didn't you say?"

"I did."

"Then counting both coming here and returning, Doctor, and killing Laura, I had something under two minutes in which to set the suicide scene, to control my apparently shattered nerves and breathing and start singing 'Berceuse'?"

Her laugh had the artificial clarity of tinkling glass.

"No, Miss Everett, it wasn't like that. You dared not risk a single gesture after your sister was dead. Your entrance into the music room had to be on time. You set the stage for suicide *after I drove you home*, while Mary lit the fire, while Dune was playing Debussy, while you were presumably arranging a tray that had already been arranged. Nobody could have entered your sister's room after we reached the house but you."

"Nobody did, Doctor. I saw her body from the door." (The break came like a rush of logs that stir, then tumble, when the jam is broken, with a turbulent stream. Her words, Starr thought, were like such logs, pelting and grinding in the savagery of their release.) "I shall drive you from this town. I'll sue you for every cent you possess. Your vile slander means nothing. You cannot prove a thing."

"I think we can. The little things were plain. For example, your scream when you pretended to find your sister dead, when you presumably had paused in her doorway to see whether she were awake, on your way back from the pantry with the drinks. It was a scream pitched to the sudden reaction to violent shock, and still no drop of liquid had been spilled from the filled glasses which were on the tray in your hand."

"Do you build your case on that, Doctor?"

"These, as I say, are the minor things. For another example, the gas. If, as we were supposed to think, your sister had committed suicide by gas the whole house would have been filled with it. She had been dead, you know, for about three hours before we got here."

She stirred slightly, and her breathing became more quick.

"You accuse me on the basis of the strength, or lack of strength, of the smell of gas? Gas seeping from a room that was tightly closed?"

Starr swung, with a pitying reluctance, his masked battery into line.

"Your sister herself accuses you, Miss Everett. Not I."

"Laura—the dead?"

"You should have left her body lying on its face."

"Is this some abortive trap, Doctor?"

"No. Things happen when a person dies, Miss Everett. The blood stops circulating, you see, and it settles gradually through the force of gravity until it becomes congested in the body's lower parts. The time varies that it takes to do so. But it, this settling, is usually completed within two or three hours. Do you begin to understand?"

She said nothing but stared up at him with bleak, puzzled eyes, while her tongue crept out to give moisture to her drying lips.

"Surely you see the picture?" Starr went on. "Your sister died with her body face downward and remained in that position for several hours, for long enough for the blood to have settled and to have established lividities that were unquestionably indicative of that position. That's why I knew you had set the scene, Miss Everett, because when I examined your sister right after you pretended to have discovered her death *every indication, every lividity and suggillation for the position in which the body lay was exactly reversed.*"

* * * *

Starr drove Dune home. He listened to a good many of Dune's "Oh Gods" before telling him flatly to shut up, because Mary was with them, still trembling and cold and sick with shock, sitting there between them on the glove-soft leather, while a paling moon brushed silver across the bordering trees.

He said to Mary, after Dune had been dropped to "Oh God" himself into a tortured bed, "I liked her voice."

"Roger's mother?"

"Yes. You can tell about people from their voices, even over a telephone. She's all right."

"I know just what you mean. I knew that the first time I heard Roger's—"

Good, Starr thought, I won't have to give her a sedative. She'll do. She'll sleep.

THE CASE OF THE
BUTTONED COLLAR

Six people were involved, if you counted the one who was killed. Against them stood the law while, between, there was Dr. Colin Starr.

On January eleventh at 9 A.M. Mrs. Beckfort did not see the smoke. The windows of her room looked backward toward the hills, the rugged hills of southeastern Ohio at the foot of which the town lay, Laurel Falls, on the bank of the Muskingum River. It was the sole room in the spacious house which she had retained for her own use. The rest, with their elegance polished to the bone, were occupied by paying guests. Elsa had been born in it twenty-two years ago, and Mrs. Beckfort's husband, Arthur, with his gentle vagaries and inspired lack of the slightest sense, had died in it with diminishing splendor seven years back.

The smoke was not there by ten.

Panic seized Mrs. Beckfort at eleven o'clock and she dialed the telephone which rested on a stand within reach of her wheel chair. An impersonally courteous voice said: "Doctor Starr's secretary speaking."

"Miss Wadsworth, this is Mrs. Beckfort. May I speak with the doctor, please?"

"Certainly, Mrs. Beckfort."

Even over the wire Starr's voice kept its friendly ability to reassure her instantly, as it always had, bulwarking her morale through the lean last years.

"Good morning."

"Oh, good morning, Doctor."

"Are the knees bothering you again?"

"No, you'll think me terribly silly, but it's Elsa."

"Yes?"

"You see, there was no smoke."

Starr knew what, she meant. It was a ritual, the smoke between Mrs. Beckfort's daughter Elsa and herself. Simple and direct as all things were which dealt with wilderness (not wilderness, exactly, but a place removed from the accessories of society such as electricity and the telephone), the signal smoke at nine every morning had been a greeting to Mrs. Beckfort from Elsa and an assurance that all was well. The habit had started a year ago when Elsa had married Joel Durban and they'd gone to live in a cabin near a forge which he'd built in the hills. Joel turned out wrought-iron objects at the forge with, Starr always thought, a plethora of muscular strength and little else.

He said: "But wouldn't Joel come in if anything were wrong?"

"That's it. Joel isn't out there. He went to Columbus the day before yesterday about some show he's arranging for his primitives."

"Was the smoke there yesterday morning?"

"Yes, just at nine."

"Possibly Elsa is coming to town."

"Even so, Doctor, she would have sent the signal. I'm afraid she's ill. I'm worried that there might have been an accident. The forge is so isolated, Doctor."

"I'll run out there, Mrs. Beckfort. I can leave here in about twenty minutes."

Her relief was evident.

"You'll let me know?"

"Yes, I'll let you know."

* * * *

Elsa's body lay cupped in snow, in a sheeted pocket fifteen feet beneath the lip of a path which frost had hardened into iron. No blood was on the snow. Her face, in death, glowed splotchily bright the way flesh does with freezing: a cherry red. A stand of black walnut trees brooded under flat and chill gray sky.

Starr knew the Luffberry boy fairly well, as well as you could get to know anything elementally primal. He had pulled Jeff back from typhoid late last year.

"How does it happen you were waiting here, Jeff?"

"There wasn't any smoke."

Jeff's voice was soft, oddly soft to go with his build and his face and hands which seemed blocked out in dark mahogany.

"Been here long?"

"No Doctor. Two or three minutes before you came."

"Take my car, will you? Pete's filling station has the nearest phone. Ask him to get in touch with the sheriff and coroner. You'd better wait and come back with them."

"All right, Doctor—"

"Yes?"

"The stove in the cabin's cold."

"Then she must have fallen last night, Jeff."

"It was stone cold last night."

"You were here?"

"I figured Mrs. Durban'd gone into town."

Starr started to say something but Jeff was gone, suddenly, with that animal ability of his to vanish, rather than just to move off, among the trees. Starr found toe holds down the steep cliff. The hard surface of the ground told him nothing when he reached it. No footprints broke the flat of surrounding snow patches, and his own were the first to cut the one where Elsa lay.

Yes, he thought, that was all right. Slipped on the path and landed down here on her back. Knocked unconscious. Then the cold had got her, caught her easily as it did the habitually ill-nourished and, as he knew her to be, the worn-out with fatigue. Lethargy would have overpowered her before she had revived, then coma and, in it, death.

A metallic firmness of her flesh assured him nothing could be done. A certain difference about her appearance disturbed him: a difference between the way he usually had seen Elsa Durban and as he saw her now, a certain neatness about the jacket, the collar being buttoned primly up about her throat (that was it) and it had always been with a loosely worn woolen scarf that Starr remembered her when out of doors. He undid the high collar. Its upper edge had pressed snugly just below her chin, and like her face (his eyes grew sharp with shock) the smooth, stiffened throat showed cherry-red marks too…

Sheriff Dixlow had received his appointment largely from his political abilities rather than through any aptitude or experience in the solution of obscure crimes. His voice especially was freighted with a valuable (politically) charm: a curiously sensitive instrument housed in a large and rather gloomy shell. He arrived with Jeff Luffberry and two deputies. He was moderately annoyed at the physical inconvenience of having to descend the cliff. He was definitely annoyed at the bitter cold. He had every intention of getting this business through quick.

"The coroner could not come, Doctor. He's in bed with a touch of flu. Your report will cover things. Start getting her up the cliff, men. She slipped on that path, fell, froze to death. That's right, Doctor?"

Starr idly watched one deputy fasten ropes. He saw the other deputy and Jeff Luffberry up on the path, waiting to haul the body up. Jeff's face was rigid and there seemed no sense in his eyes.

"I suggest that one of your deputy coroners make an examination," Starr said.

"Really? Why?"

Starr held his voice low.

"I think Mrs. Durban was killed and that her body was then dropped from the path onto the snow. It's simply an opinion which I would prefer to have one of your men decide for himself."

Dixlow viewed this thoughtfully from the political vantage points and decided to be pleased. Starr followed the workings of his mind: a woman of no importance (Dixlow would be thinking) but one whose family had been socially and financially prominent in the life of Laurel Falls; color, too, in this business of her husband hammering out those iron things, the Bohemian touch. Sure to be a good press, and certainly the setup seemed simple enough. Dixlow's brooding eyes traveled slowly upward toward the path. They came to rest on young Luffberry and stayed there.

"He was on the scene when you got here, wasn't he, Doctor?"

"Yes."

Dixlow said, "Hmmmmmm."

The deputies took Elsa Durban's body into Laurel Falls in Dixlow's car. He himself (now that he was in for it) intended to go in with Starr after he'd looked things over. Things and Jeff Luffberry. He wanted Jeff to show him just what he'd done when he found the stove cold that morning and when he'd found it cold the night before.

The cabin was icy. There were three rooms. The front and only door opened into a general living room. Two doors in this room led into a kitchen and a bedroom. There were four windows: two in the living room and one each in the kitchen and bedroom. All were shut.

The furniture and arrangement were crudely individual except for the cook-stove. The woodwork had been hewn and fashioned by Joel Durban's muscular hands, the utensils pounded out by him at the adjacent forge.

Dixlow's body brooded like a grim and forceful shadow beside the frigid cook-stove, while his utterly charming and cultured voice went on with its questions.

"How long have you known the Durbans, Mr. Luffberry?"

"Since soon after they came here, Sheriff."

"You work on the Fenner farm, don't you, over on the main road?"

"Yes."

"Had you known the Durbans before they settled here?"

"No. I gave him a hand when he put up the forge."

"I see. And the friendship ripened?"

"I helped now and then. When he was away. She wasn't very strong."

"Not much of a life for her here, I imagine, When you consider her background."

"She never said."

"But you could see?"

"Anybody could see, Sheriff."

Starr recognized the trend, a quiet stalking on velvet pads toward the commonplace crime of passion: young Luffberry's untamed virility, Elsa's charm, her interest in him, her occasional dependence on him during Joel's absences. And the thing that disturbed him most was that psychologically the motive, in Jeff's case, might be sound; the motive, but not the method with which he believed that Mrs. Durban had been put to death.

He said, "I've known Mrs. Durban rather well for a good many years, Sheriff. I think I can assure you that her devotion for her husband was exceptional."

"Exceptional?"

"In its strength, Sheriff. She loved him so completely that no one else, that nothing else seemed to exist."

Dixlow smiled.

"I'm glad you told me that, Doctor." He stared with an impersonal insolence at Jeff, neatly arranging in his mind the familiar recipe, and then said, "We know that Mrs. Durban was alive at nine o'clock yesterday morning when her mother, Mrs. Beckfort, saw the signal smoke. According to your story, Mr. Luffberry, you came here at seven last night and found the stove cold. You thought that Mrs. Durban had gone into town. You returned this morning when you failed to sec the signal smoke and, becoming worried, you searched the woods, the paths, and found Mrs. Durban's body. Why were you worried, Mr. Luffberry? What caused you to change your opinion that she had simply gone into town and was presumably staying with her mother?"

"You wouldn't understand."

"On the contrary, I've the most open sort of a mind. You've told us that everything here was in order, nothing upset, the bed neatly made, the dishes, the cooking things clean; was it just a presentiment, Mr. Luffberry?"

"Yes. I knew she was dead."

Dixlow stopped smiling.

"On Doctor Starr's advice I am arranging for an autopsy. Have you anything to say, Mr. Luffberry?"

"What are you getting at, Sheriff?"

"Just the facts we'll have to know eventually. Funny thing, the different ways in which a woman will react. Take the mental type like Mrs. Durban, sufficiently sophisticated, intellectual and well-bred. Did she repulse you immediately or did you both discuss the matter for a while? I mean did you have to sit here and listen to her explain this unique love, this binding sense of loyalty she felt for her husband, while your, well, more primal urges were driving you into a state of temporary insanity? I suppose that is what you *will* plead, Mr. Luffberry?"

Starr could have told him it would happen. Jeff's fist struck once, on the point of the chin, and Dixlow lay unconscious on the floor, while in the utter stillness of the icy house the sound of monotonous crying came from the living room. Starr followed Jeff in. He saw the girl sitting on a stool, her face ugly with tears.

"Hello, Martha," Jeff said. He turned to Starr. "She's the teacher in that school up the line. We're going to get married." He walked over. "Let's get going, Martha."

"I heard him, Jeff." She stopped crying long enough to stare bleakly through the bedroom doorway at Dixlow's long legs and shoes. One shoe was beginning to twitch.

"He's crazy, Martha. Why did you come here?"

"I followed you. I followed you last night."

Nothing was so trenchant as the shocks of youth, Starr thought, and she was young, a simple, pretty little thing if she'd ever stop crying, facing with no experience whatever the brutal, wrenching bewilderment of wondering whether this boy she loved, whose life she had promised to share, had betrayed a woman and killed her and in doing so had betrayed herself too.

Jeff put a hand on her shoulder. She started to shake. "I won't tell," she said, "but don't touch me." His fingers tightened and she screamed. She said, "No, no, Jeff," and sidled toward the door, looking back over a shoulder with wet, panicky eyes.

Starr said sharply, "Let her go."

"She's crazy too."

"No, she'll be all right."

They heard her stumbling through leafless brush. Then Dixlow was swaying in the bedroom doorway. He had a revolver in his hand, aiming it at young Luffberry.

"I doubt whether you'll need the gun, Sheriff," Starr said.

"Won't I?" Dixlow steadied himself with the other hand against the doorjamb. "Turn your face to the wall, Luffberry."

"The hell with you."

Dixlow fired. In the shoulder, Starr thought, was where Jeff got it, just as Jeff used his uncanny ability to vanish and leaped through the front door. Dixlow emptied his gun senselessly in a vicious rage at thick trunks of trees. He gave Starr an inimical glance.

"You were quite a help, Doctor," he said.

* * * *

Snow started falling at four. Starr assured Mrs. Pendergast that her blood pressure was under control. He agreed to a slight change in her diet: lobster by all means, if she wished, to replace fillet of sole. He said good-by. He rang for his secretary. Miss Wadsworth, thoroughly starched and white, came into the office. "Yes, Doctor?"

"Any more appointments?"

"Mrs. Pendergast was the last."

"Sit down, Miss Wadsworth."

"Thank you, Doctor."

"What have you found out?"

"The sheriff has around twenty men searching the hills. He's taken that girl Martha into custody as a material witness. He believes she saw Jeff Luffberry throw the body over the cliff. The autopsy confirms your impression that Mrs. Durban died of carbonic-oxide poisoning."

"Any signs of violence, of assault?"

"No, nothing like that. Doctor Tulson did the p.m. He said that the case would have gone through as a plain accidental death from exposure if it hadn't been for you. Incidentally the sheriff has given a complete statement covering each step of the crime. The *Sentinel* has an extra on it."

"What did he say?"

"Jeff Luffberry declared his uncontrollable passion for Mrs. Durban last night—Dixlow's own words, Doctor—and she repulsed him. She appealed to his better nature. He left."

"Oh, so he left?"

"Yes. But not for long. His better nature shortly decamped and left his baser nature holding the bag. Being well versed in chemistry—I don't imagine the poor kid knows a thing about—Jeff knew that poisoning results from the fumes of burning charcoal. Dixlow went to town about charcoal. He was beautifully pat about a charcoal fire being smoldering rather than brisk and giving off considerable quantities of carbonic monoxide. He pregnantly underlined the fact that there was plenty of charcoal piled up in Durban's forge."

"I see. Jeff came back after Elsa Durban had gone to sleep, shut the windows, filled the stove with charcoal, closed the dampers and so forth?"

"That's right. Later, after the carbonic oxide had done the trick, he came back again and threw Mrs. Durban's body over the cliff so that it would seem she had slipped and frozen to death."

"In the meanwhile," Starr said bitterly, "that youngster is loose in the hills with a slug in his shoulder from Dixlow's gun. Dixlow's a good man but he lacks control. His mind forms in patterns and stays set. How about Elsa's mother, Miss Wadsworth?"

"I phoned a quarter of an hour ago. Joel Durban is with her. He says Mrs. Beckforth is bearing up very well."

"When did he get back from Columbus?"

"About an hour ago. He found Dixlow and his men at the cabin and went out of his head for a while, according to Dixlow, from shock and grief. He came in to sec that Mrs. Beckfort was all right. Shortly he's going to join the posse and is going to kill young Luffberry."

"Where did he stay while he was in Columbus?"

"I thought you'd want to know that, Doctor. He was a guest of. Mrs. Worthington Culver. She's a wealthy society woman, a widow. She was handling his exhibition for him. Launching him, you know." Miss Wadsworth's intelligent eyes grew stark. "Doctor, isn't there anything you can do? That crowd is so stirred up and Dixlow's so convinced of his guilt that they're ready to shoot Jeff Luffberry on sight."

"Put a call through to Columbus, please. Try and get Mrs. Culver on the wire." Mrs. Worthington Culver's voice (ten minutes later) had all the assurance of middle age, social importance and great wealth.

"Doctor Starr? Something about Mr. Joel Durban, Renfrew said?" Her tone shifted into anxiety. "Was there an accident, Doctor, on his drive to Laurel Falls?"

"No, Mrs. Culver, not to him."

"To someone who was with him? I've warned Joel repeatedly about hitchhikers."

"When did he leave your house?"

"Shortly before noon."

"Do you mind my asking where he was yesterday morning at nine o'clock?"

"Joel? He was right here. We breakfasted early, *just* at nine as a matter of fact. The committee handling his exhibition met at eleven. May I ask you the meaning of these questions, Doctor?"

"Was Mr. Durban at that meeting?"

"Naturally."

"Did he leave right after it for Laurel Falls?"

Mrs. Culver's voice took on an edge.

"I've already told you that he left for Laurel Falls around noon today, *not* yesterday. He was with me constantly all of yesterday. I must insist on an explanation of this?"

"Mr. Durban's wife has been killed, Mrs. Culver."

Mrs. Culver said after a pause, "Are you certain we are speaking about the same Mr. Durban, Doctor? Joel Durban, the one who does those magnificent primitives in wrought iron?"

"Yes, that's right."

"And you did say his—wife?"

"Yes."

There was a longer pause still.

"I suppose you are in touch with Mr. Durban, Doctor?"

"I expect to see him very soon."

"Then will you offer him my condolences, please?"

"Certainly."

"Also"—Mrs. Culver's laugh was definitive and brief—"my regrets."

The line clicked, and Starr smiled faintly at Miss Wadsworth.

"The usual perfect alibi," he said.

"Had you seriously considered Mr. Durban, Doctor? I mean, he and Elsa, everyone felt it one of those blinding things, a real, a deep, true love match, if that isn't slopping over into mawkishness."

"No, things don't happen like that. Nature abhors, biologically, a balance. One love invariably is the stronger of a two, flames actively like a fire near which the other basks, finds warmth—a fire—" Starr's virile, pleasant face hardened into thoughtful lines. He said abruptly, "Call Mrs. Beckfort's house, please. Get Durban on the wire."

Within the twenty minutes which it took for Joel Durban to leave Mrs. Beckfort's and reach Starr's office Starr did three things. The first consisted in a phone call to District Attorney Heffernan. It occupied a full ten minutes and hauled Mr. Heffernan's temperature from iced skepticism up to a fever of promised activity.

The second was brief. He phoned the *Sentinel* and asked for their weather forecast of the day before yesterday. It had read: *Cloudy, with increasing cold.*

The third consisted in asking Miss Wadsworth to run upstairs to his dressing room and get his revolver from the small right-hand bureau drawer. Starr placed the revolver on his desk. He selected two instruments from a cabinet in the operating room. He returned to the desk.

He said to Miss Wadsworth, "Once upon a time a blind man stood on the lip of a precipice and, as he thought, his sight was miraculously restored. The man turned his back upon the chasm and saw before him three paths, and a voice said to him: one of these paths will lead you backward along your life to safety." Starr smiled at the frightened look on Miss Wadsworth's wholesome, matter-of-fact face. "No, I haven't

gone mad. I'm simply wondering which path he will choose."   J o e l
Durban came into the office a few minutes before five.

Early dark of winter had blotted out the day, and two lamps glowed
in the shadowed room. Starr was impressed, as he habitually found himself so, by the magnificent physique and classical perfection of features
with which young Durban was accustomed to stun (in varying degrees
of force) the members of either sex. He also caught the radiation of
Durban's equally magnificent conceit and self-centered assurance that
the world was a better and certainly a more pictorial place because he,
Durban, was in it. Starr offered his condolences. He asked Durban to sit
down.

He said, "I thought you would like to know, Joel, that Elsa didn't
suffer. I can assure you of that."

A faint tightness about Durban's handsome eyes smoothed from
relief.

"Thank you, Doctor."

"It occurred to me that you would also like to know just how things
stand."

Durban's look flicked casually toward the revolver which lay beneath a partially masking sheet of note paper on the desk top.

"I do know, Doctor."

"Oh, then you've heard from District Attorney Heffernan?"

The tightness returned.

"Heffernan?"

"Yes. He phoned me shortly before you came. About that girl the
sheriff's holding, about Martha."

"Yes?"

"She thinks now that she made a mistake. That's natural when you
consider she was driven into hysteria and that her nerves are still fairly
shot."

"Then she didn't see anything after all?"

"Oh yes, she saw something all right, something which she claims
is just on the fringe of her memory and which any moment may make
quite clear. But she thinks her mistake was in the time. Whatever this
was that she saw she now says that she didn't see it last night. She saw
it the night before."

Durban said quickly, "That's impossible, Doctor. Elsa was alive yesterday morning. She lighted the signal fire yesterday morning."

"Heffernan was puzzled by that too. He feels that unless Martha is
more than ever confused by hysteria there are two possibilities about that
fire. He thinks young Luffberry may have set it himself to delay a search

for Elsa, which doesn't make much sense, or else that some sort of a time-bomb device was used."

Durban's voice was careful.

"Has he talked this over with the sheriff?"

"No, he only thought of it a quarter of an hour ago when he was questioning Martha at Dixlow's house."

"House? Isn't she being held in the county jail?"

"No, she's with Mrs. Dixlow. They thought it better for Martha's nerves, that a clear memory of whatever it was she saw on the night before last would return to her more quickly. Heffernan's looking into that fire business in the morning, going to have the ashes sifted, that sort of thing."

Durban stood up, towered handsomely in the glow from the desk lamp.

"I'll take it up with the sheriff myself. I'm going out to the cabin now to join the search."

"Be careful, Joel."

"Don't worry."

"Have you a gun?"

"No. I'll get one from the sheriff."

"Take mine. I had planned to be with the posse, but a case is keeping me in town."

Durban pocketed the revolver.

"Thanks, Doctor."

(*Three paths*, thought Starr, *and one led to a youngster bleeding like a shot animal in some fastness of the hills, and one led to dead ashes of a fire, while the last led toward that bourne from which—*)

* * * *

The shot cracked crisply in the chill night air, and the scene arranged in the lighted window of the living room of Dixlow's house changed slowly according to plan. Martha's hands clasped spasmodically on her breast and she sank forward in the chair and toppled onto the floor.

Starr moved with Heffernan from behind a masking spruce and they blocked young Durban as he rose from a crouch. Durban looked at them stupidly, while the revolver swung loosely from a finger of his right hand. He started to cry. He said, in a welter of self-pity, "There was so little time. It was hard to figure what ought to be done first."

Starr said equably, "Panic does that to people, Joel. Like drowning, they grasp what's near at hand. Like drivers who hit and run, panic arouses their instinct for self-preservation to the deadening of everything else. You thought it better to come here first and shoot Martha before she could remember the things you imagined she had seen. Then would be time enough to destroy whatever mechanism you had arranged at the signal fire, and lastly you could take care of Jeff. Were you going to fix things so that it would seem to have been he who shot Martha and then that he had killed himself?"

Durban's voice stayed stupid, thick.

"Yes, Doctor—there seemed a way—such quantities of time left through the night."

"Tell me, why did you kill Elsa? Naturally we realize you intended to marry Mrs. Culver and her wealth and that her interest in you would have deadened if she'd known you had a wife, but after all, there is the mechanism of divorce. Tell me really why, Joel?"

Durban's handsome eyes were wide with candor. He said with the utmost conviction, "But I never could have just *left* Elsa, Doctor. It would have killed her. Don't you see?"

It was easier then. He told them just what he had done: how he'd come back from Columbus the night before last and killed Elsa with the charcoal fumes while she lay in the deep first hours of sleep and then dressed her and thrown her body over the cliff; told them of the time bomb for the fire which he'd made at the forge, of the weather forecast which had assured him there would be no snowfall to smother the fire. Then he said bitterly, "Why did you let me shoot Martha? It was such a useless thing when you already knew."

"There's no hole in the glass of that window, Joel. I took the lead from the bullets before I gave you the gun."

There was something that Durban still sought in the deep confusion of his mind. He said to Starr, "But at the first, when you found Elsa—I looked it up in a medical book in the library—if anyone freezes to death their skin gets a cherry red, just as it does if they die from the fumes of charcoal—it was so foolproof—how did you know?"

Starr felt, against reason, a sense of pity.

"It's a case of the little knowledge being a dangerous thing, Joel. The flesh in both instances docs turn a cherry red, but with freezing, the only parts that do so are those *which have been exposed to the air*. Your mistake, when you dressed Elsa, lay in buttoning the collar of her coat."

* * * *

They brought young Luffberry in around midnight. Starr was waiting in the cabin, with Miss Wadsworth, dressings, probes and Martha Dean. They'd found Jeff unconscious in a cave further back in the hills. It was a flesh wound of, as Starr had thought, the shoulder. It did not worry Starr or Martha or Jeff himself when he came to. Because, as all three of them knew, young Luffberry was tough.

THE CASE OF THE LONELY LADIES

CHAPTER 1

She held the letter in her hands for a long time, thinking, while her dark eyes stared from under fine lashes through a window that was sullen beneath murky overtones of a threatening storm. She felt wretchedly chilled and nervous, in a way that she hadn't known for years. It was of small moment in itself, the letter, but it served to bring her problems to a sharp focus and to set a period mark on any further procrastination.

Extrasensory phenomena had never been considered by her in one way or another, for plainer terms such as moods, hunches were more to her liking. She was experiencing one then: a sense of disaster (she went further in a rush of self-honesty and labeled it danger), and she was too clever a woman to dismiss the feeling without making an effort to trace it to its source. There was, that she could discover, absolutely none.

Her name was Lily Elser.

That was it: it was sixteen years ago when she had felt like this, during the first few weeks when she had come to Ohio and settled down in Laurel Falls with her daughter Nan, who had then been a child of three. Lily herself was at the time only twenty-two, but a certain maturity of manner had made her seem older. It had stamped her with a quality of agelessness which had never changed and without detracting in any fashion from the warm charm of her character and pleasant looks.

As there had not been the least reason for anyone to be curious about them her antecedents prior to Laurel Falls had been initially obscure. It was generally understood that they involved several cities which were as far-flung as Seattle and New Orleans, with brief sojourns at St Paul and Pittsburgh in between. Lily had been accepted without the slightest curiosity as a delightful young widow whose name had then been Mrs. Robert Warden.

There had been enough money for Lily to engage an agreeable suite in the Mansion House, and she had ascribed her decision to remain there simply to the natural beauties of Laurel Falls, which lay in the ruggedly hilly southeastern portion of Ohio, on the banks of the Onega River. Unobtrusively and always with a correct sense of reticence she had found her way into the social life of the community. Her regular Sunday attendance with Nan at All-Saints-in-the-Valley had with time brought her many agreeable contacts which later developed into sincere friendships.

It was predestined, of course, that she would marry again. Completely apart from any mental or physical qualities Lily belonged to that fairly rare stamp of women who are, inescapably, wives. Without in the least being helpless she did suggest an impression of being so. There was nothing conscious or deliberate about this on her part: it just was there as a fact, and every man felt it and instantly started in figuring out ways for helping and protecting her.

Lily had come with the years to know that look. To recognize it the instant it sparked in a man's eye and then spread out into a warm, protective glow.

Faintly she resented it for she knew herself to be sane, sound and capable, with strengths that could (and had) cope efficiently with varied emergencies. But she could not, in the kindness of her heart, ever bring herself to the point of quenching it. Never, certainly, before the glow was fixed, and then it was always too late.

Milton Elser had had it seven years ago, so Lily had married him and had moved with Nan from the Mansion House and into Elser's spacious home on Onega Drive. It was a small estate, really, for the property extended in the rear to the bank of the river and was masked from the main highway in front by broad landscaped lawns dotted with metal fauna elegancies of the day. The buildings, which included stables and a gate lodge, were in the handsomest tradition of Stanford White, and the three of them lived there in an even state of unexciting contentment with Elser daily protecting and cosseting Lily and she letting herself be both and Nan getting finished at the Misses Tunkets' in Maryland.

There was this to be said for the firmness with which Lily's roots had struck into the town's society. Nobody for a minute considered that she might have married Milton Elser for his money, and this in spite of the fact that Elser was a good twenty years her senior. There had seemed a rightness about the match: a satisfactory exchange of security for Lily and Nan and of an agreeable companionship and shepherding rights for Elser.

Then Elser had died.

This was several months ago after a full year's distressing illness which had terminated in a stroke, leaving Elser helplessly bedridden until his death. So there was Lily a widow again, alone with Nan, and the sole mistress of an estate which the town felt certain must be very large.

It wasn't.

Elser's malady had been seated in the brain, and long before his stroke his judgment had begun to falter, a condition that was aggravated by a dread on his part that he would die and Lily would be left unsheltered, a tragic, tender sheep alone among the financial wolves and morasses of the world's unsettled state. He had viewed the collapse of great houses, of guaranteed mortgage bonds (and similar once-invincible solaces for widows, idiots and orphans), and his tired, kindly head got completely muddled.

As a result Elser had converted a fortune in reasonably sound holdings into a myriad of desperate eggs for whose goodness and hatching he would develop some transiently intensive hope. He had specifically barred any sale of the estate during Lily's lifetime (always she must have shelter, a roof and warmth and light and things to eat), then had lumped the whole sorry mess into a trust and had wished it on the First National Bank of Laurel Falls as both executors and trustees. For Lily.

Lily turned from the window with dread. It was a dread at the immediate steps which she would have to set into motion. All of her life she had disliked an air of tolerance, and Sheffield would, she knew, continue to be tolerant. Sheffield and Delilah both. They were part of the estate, having started in service with Elser's parents, whom they had respectfully wept into their graves, and continued through Elser, weeping him into his grave, and would undoubtedly (Lily felt) weep her into hers. They were, of course, the type of Negroes who never, never die. Lily had found it difficult to be firm with them and impossible to be hard, and now she might have to be both.

She left the living room with its fine old things and went through a broad hallway to the quarters in the rear. Sheffield and Delilah both stood up with gracious politeness when she came into the roomy kitchen. A rabbit casserole was fragrant on the range, and the air was pungent with the tang of baking bread. Lily's nervousness increased and her fingers were chilled. She thought for a wretched moment that they might begin to tremble, like impossibly flexible icicles in a wind. She came straight to the point.

"I'm considering taking in tourists, Sheffield. If the plan is agreeable to the trustees I'll arrange with Bellamy's after lunch to place a signboard at the gates."

He said, "We was afraid."

"There's nothing else I can do."

"No'm, we was aware of that."

Probably, Lily thought, before she had been aware of it herself. Well, there *wasn't* anything else either. But this immediate capitulation surprised her until she reflected that it was based on an acceptance of overnight tourists as the lesser evil of possible others.

There were the things. Heirlooms of Sheraton, of Phyfe, some good glass, some silver. There were also the paintings: a fine Benjamin West, a Vanderlin, a Rembrandt Peale, some lesser fry, but all of a certain value to a collector of Americana. Yes, therein lay their greater evil: she might have sold something or persuaded the trustees, rather, to permit her to do so. Sold some of the heirlooms out of the family, which was dead but which didn't matter because in the opinion of Sheffield and Delilah the Elsers continued to own them in some supernal fashion, whereas Lily only lived among them on a slender tenure of (still supernal) sufferance.

Oddly she thought: And they're quite right.

She said to Delilah, "Some of the bedrooms might be made ready. There isn't much traffic in winter, so I doubt whether we'll need more than a few."

Delilah's origin was Jamaica, and she had never lost the soft, slurred flavor of her English. She said, "Is it satisfactory to Madam to use the ones in the north wing?"

"Yes, those, please, Delilah."

"Will there be meals served too, madam?"

Lily had wondered about that. She thought not. The first step alone was difficult enough of itself. And still it seemed stupid to hang suspended in the center of a plunge.

"Perhaps morning coffee and toast, Delilah, and fruit juice, in their rooms."

"Yes, madam. That can be done. And the silver?"

"Silver?"

"Will you wish us to put it away?"

It came back to Lily swiftly and more strongly, that foreboding sense of danger, and this time she could label it quite simply: Taking strangers into the house.

"Thank you, Delilah, for thinking of it. It would be best."

She left the kitchen and got ready to drive down to the bank. The thought stayed with her while she did so, expanding across a canvas that grew ever more somber: the potential dangers of the step she was planning, which so many hard-pressed women had been compelled to take before her.

A tourist house was different from hotels. Hotels had staffs, house detectives, any number of protective measures both for sizing up their guests and for coping with any eventuality whatever. But with a private house which was suddenly thrown open to the public—

Lily cut the thought off sharply, settling a smart hat, arranging furs, thinking of her mirrored face and expensive turnout in the uncertain terms of a whited sepulcher, uncertain because she had never been sure as to what the phrase definitely meant, but she felt it analogous to false western fronts.

* * * *

Mr. Lorrimer Keith was, for the president of a bank, a young man, scarcely five or six years older than Lily herself. But then, the First National of Laurel Falls was a family affair almost to the point of being entailed. Groton and Williams, also entailed, had done their customary job and had sent him back to Ohio, a finished product of their personal tradition.

He cordially detested everything about banking and would have given anything to have outfitted a caravan and toured the countryside, presenting plays of an intimate, intensive nature in an intimate and intensive way. A yearning, he knew, utterly vain, for his body belonged to Laurel Falls no matter where his soul might long to flit, just as the bodies of his ancestors had belonged to Laurel Falls before him. And whatever might churn inside of it his shell was a beautifully glazed example of courteous business acumen and sound Rotary Club restraint.

He had gone through one brief and disastrous marriage, a rebellious gambol in reality among his secret Elysian fields, with a girl from New York's Greenwich Village. And Genevieve had certainly brought life to Laurel Falls. Then, after busting up two families and giving a local welterweight ideas (finer things in life—the brain—a touch of soul, of poetry above the belt) Genevieve had got a divorce and had returned, plus alimony, to Greenwich Village. Leaving Keith in a daze of unspeakable relief.

He caught Lily on her way to the paying teller and led her across polished marble into his office. He had always liked Lily enormously, because he thought her decorative and knew her to be both intelligent and nice. Well, and comfortable too. Flow, immeasurably so, he often thought, in comparison with his yardstick Genevieve. Recently, since he had found himself in the role of chief trustee to the Elser estate, he had worried about Lily terrifically, because he knew down to a penny the muddled financial abyss which Elser had left her in. He seated her with a Clyde Fitch flourish in an armchair and offered her a cigarette.

"We see too little of you, Lily."

She smiled and said, "I've so little to come here for, Lorrimer."

"I know, and I've been wondering."

"What recipe I'll use for cooking the wolf?"

"Yes. The best thing to do. We've got to tide you over, Lily."

He stared at her earnestly, and Lily thought uncomfortably: It's there. The look. She couldn't mistake it after so much experience through the years with its inevitable kindling, the glint, which would so shortly spread into the warmly protective glow. Right now, she decided, was the instant to quench it (just as she had always decided) but she couldn't bring herself to do so, any more than she had been able to in the past.

Keith was saying, "I can't take the securities as collateral for a loan without having the bank examiners bring charges of lunacy and embezzlement. I don't think they're utterly worthless, but that's just my private opinion. I think the coal stocks especially will be all right after this strike nonsense is settled. We can't touch the house or grounds, of course, but that doesn't matter. I doubt whether you could even give the place away for taxes as things are now. Lily"—Keith hesitated uncomfortably—"you need cash. You need it for food and fuel. You need it to carry you until, well, the mines start paying again. I want you to let me take that stock over. Just a transfer sale, and later I'll sell it back to you."

She felt the sting of tears at the genuine warmth of his friendliness, at this interest in her concern.

"Thank you, Lorrimer, but I've thought of a way."

"What is it, Lily?"

"I came here really to see you about it. To find out whether legally I've the right to do it. I want to turn the place into a tourist house, if that's permissible under the trust."

He sensed a firmness in her, a firmness against his stock-transfer idea or any other idea which would simply be a euphemism for a personal loan. He thought of how rigidly the old conventions still retained their bonds.

"Lily, I don't like it."

"I don't myself especially, but what is there else?"

"I don't know. It's the usual solution, heaven knows, either tourists or boarders. There, Lily, why not boarders? People you know? At least they're—well—safe."

"But I *would* know them, Lorrimer. That's just it."

She touched, against her own convictions, on mountains and molehills, her decided preference in opening the house to strangers rather than to the permanence of acquaintances, the worries and eventual irritations of having them rooted beneath the roof. She asked again her legal status on the subject.

"Why surely, Lily, that end of it's all right. You can do anything on earth with the place except mortgage it or sell it. Lily—how are things now? At this minute, I mean?"

"Nan wrote me this morning that she needs money. I'm drawing fifty and wiring it to her."

Keith shoved a checkbook across the desk and handed her a pen. He knew her balance to be around ninety-two dollars. An idea occurred to him and he felt immeasurably easier.

"Look here, I've got it. I'll fix up a chattel mortgage on some of the stuff. That's something we can do. Just a small one, Lily, for running expenses right now."

There it was: the things. But it wasn't like selling them, and after some income started coming in, and after all, there was no other instant solution to (she admitted it) almost instant starvation and penury.

"Just a very small one, Lorrimer?"

"Very small. What's Nan's address in Detroit? I'll take care of the wire for you."

"Thank you. She's staying at the Otis House."

Lily gave him the address and wrote out the check.

Keith said diffidently, "How's Nan doing, Lily?"

Her eyes were suddenly bleak.

"I don't know. I made her promise to write if she needed money. That's all I know, Lorrimer."

"You do love her an awful lot, don't you, Lily? I don't blame you. Nan's one of the nicest girls I know. I've wondered—"

He stopped abruptly and Lily said, "You've wondered what, Lorrimer?"

"I'm sorry, because it's none of my business, except that I like Nan so much. I've wondered about Gene Forrest. Nobody could help seeing how far he was gone on Nan, and I rather thought she felt the same way about him."

Lily's expression changed subtly. Keith thought of it like something warm and fluid which all of a sudden hardens. It made him think of a movie show he had once been at when the machine suddenly stopped turning and left him there, looking at a still.

"Gene is so young, Lorrimer," Lily said.

"He's twenty-four."

"That's young." She repeated the word with almost a stubborn fierceness. "Young."

"Well, I'm sorry if I brought it up. I'll get the papers ready. This is Friday. May I come up on Monday for you to sign them?"

"Of course, Lorrimer."

"In the evening?"

"Surely, if you wish."

They stood up, and Keith escorted her to the door of the bank. He stood watching her as she moved through the gloomy light and got into her car and drove away. He thought that that *was* why Lily had let Nan go to Detroit and become a stylist or window decorator or whatever it was: to get her away from Gene Forrest. It didn't make sense.

Gene was all right. He was fine. His family was all right and he had cut out all his youthful capers and was doing a good job in Hendrickson's law office and would someday be making real money. That was a funny crack about Gene being too young. Lily had meant it too. Now if Gene had been a lot older that would have made her attitude more reasonable.

Keith fleetingly hoped that Lily wasn't going Russian in any morbidly inverted sense, the sort that was so impregnated in their plays. There was steel in her all right, laced through her lovely helpless softnesses. He'd rarely felt anything so inflexible as her attitude about Nan and Gene, and it was also there in her determination to go in for that hazardous bedding down of strangers. Well (he turned and presented his president face to the bank), you certainly never could tell about women.

Mrs. Moltenborry, one of their heaviest depositors, said for the second time, "It looks like a storm, Mr. Keith."

Keith stared at her vacantly, beamed and floated on. She thought it a shame.

* * * *

Snow fell on Saturday.

Gene Forrest called on Lily during the afternoon. He had grown to consider his twenty-four years; since settling down at law at Hendrickson's, as middle age. His face had a healthy Scotch look, wind-burned and full of heather, for he managed to get in considerable skiing and skating when not chasing around serving summonses or doing the dreary spadework on briefs. The tourist sign at the gates as he had been driving past the Elser estate had hit him like a blow. He just had to go in.

Sheffield smiled at him with pleasure as he took Gene's hat and coat. Lily, in the living room, smiled at him, too, but not with so much apparent pleasure. Gene felt foolish now that he was inside and actually sitting down beside her. What could you say, except that he had seen the sign?

He said, "I saw the sign, Mrs. Elser."

"Oh, yes. Then the snow hasn't covered it?"

"No, it's perfectly plain."

"I had thought it might. A blizzard feeling, don't you think?"

"Maybe. It's little snow, very fine. It could turn into a blizzard."

He felt hot and stuff, and his wind burn reddened more deeply. There were moments in a man's life when you either exploded or didn't, so he exploded. "Mrs. Elser, why don't you like me?"

"But I do, Gene. I mean I've nothing whatever against you."

"That's a funny way of putting it. I don't mean to be rude, Mrs. Elser. You know that."

"Of course, Gene."

"Everybody knows that the estate, well, wasn't what everybody thought it was, but that sign, I mean nobody ever thought it was as bad as that. You can't *do* it, Mrs. Elser."

His intensity bewildered Lily.

"Tourists, Gene? They're nothing to take so desperately."

"No, Mrs. Elser, not tourists. Nan."

"What on earth has Nan got to do with it?"

"You shan't sacrifice her. I won't let you."

It had been a nervous, tiring day, and Lily's head ached badly. She could not, she thought, put up with a scene that was evidently to be predicated upon the emotional tempests of young (and thwarted) love. She saw the synopsis, of course, in Gene's earnest nut-brown eyes beneath their sun-and snow-bleached lashes: herself a tyrant mother offering Nan at the altar of some suitable, wealthy match, grinding the petals of true young love beneath the excuse of knowing what was best. Well, her head was in far too bad a state for any scene like that.

She said, "I know what you're thinking, Gene, and it's silly. I've no intention of forcing Nan into a rich match even if I could. Nan has an excellent mind of her own."

"Then what was the matter with *me*?" It was a relief in a way to get down to brass tacks like this, after weeks and weeks of doubt and worry and of not knowing why or what. "Nan loved me, Mrs. Elser."

"Did she say so?"

"No. I never asked her. I didn't have to ask her, Mrs. Elser." He added miserably, "You sent her to Detroit."

"Gene, you must excuse me but I'm not feeling very well. I gave Nan permission to go to Detroit. I didn't send her. You must believe that and, as I say, excuse me."

He stood up, and his face was no longer ruddy but pretty white.

"You've got to forgive me for busting in like this. Maybe I was wrong. You get to thinking things are so sometimes just because you want them to be."

He held out his hand.

"Good-by, Gene."

"Good-by, Mrs. Elser."

Lily felt empty and sad and lonely when Gene was gone, in the way she supposed all mothers must feel when they've had the miserable satisfaction of doing something which they know is right. Having forgotten (she supposed this too) their own young assurances and fierce wants in the mellow smugness of the simple fact of maternity and the broadening, deadening wisdom that had come with age.

The snow fell all through the dreary afternoon, muffling and whitening the earth, and Sheffield said to Lily as he served dinner, "I've done turned on the light, ma'am."

"Light?"

"On the signboard, ma'am."

"Oh. Thank you, Sheffield."

Of course Bellamy's would have arranged a light when they had put the board up in the morning. So that the sign could be read by strangers who passed in the storm. It chilled Lily faintly to realize that the die was so definitely cast, that at any moment at all, from right now on all through the dark long night the bell might ring and a stranger would walk in with the right to pay for shelter, to go upstairs and do all of the things which were so commonplace in a guest: bathe, undress, go to bed.

Wander.

The word stuck, but Lily forced herself to think it out: wander about the house at night, perhaps leave it, on some mission which would be beyond her privilege to know, and then come back. In all the silent loneliness of the endless hours of the night the house would be the stranger's to do in what he pleased.

The last mail came at nine. There was a letter in it from Nan, very brief, oddly restrained: the wire for fifty had been received; there were thanks, a warmingly deep expression of love and a completely obscure sentence which read, "Things just do happen, don't they, Mother?" Across the bottom were the usual scratches of crosses, only there were more of them, and Lily thought they seemed feverish and as if they'd been crossed on in haste. Her head hurt as if it would split.

It snowed through Sunday, and by Monday a gale was whipping it into a blizzard, grounding all planes, blocking roads and thoroughly disrupting traffic. The afternoon held the somber qualities of night.

The doorbell rang at four.

* * * *

The stranger stood up as Lily entered the living room.

She saw that Sheffield had taken his hat and coat, leaving him a dark, stocky man in a pin-striped serge suit that slipped over the border line of conservative tailoring. Lily thought of his black hair as having a gangster gloss, and she thought that he could not spend very much of his time in the sun. His eyes, as she advanced closer to him, became more penetrating, and their expression of sharp concentration did not change as he held out his hand and his lips widened into a smile over strong, good teeth.

"Mrs. Elser? My name is Parne. Chester Parne. It's quite a storm, isn't it? I didn't know you caught them like this in Ohio."

Lily took his hand, finding it cold and hard in, curiously, a lifeless sort of way.

"We've had more snow this winter than in a good many years, Mr. Parne." (What on earth did you say next? Baldly, the price? She had come to think during Saturday and Sunday and the earlier parts of to-day—all of which had been void of tourists—that none would apply, that the plan was a dud: a blessing that was far from being unmixed.) "Won't you sit down?"

"Thank you." Parne arranged himself with initial formality in a brocaded lounge chair, lifting his trouser legs to preserve their creases, then carefully placing his white, manicured fingers on his knees. "I hope you've room for me."

"Of course."

"Thank you. I'm heading East, but I ask you!"

His gesture encompassed impassable drifts and the biting, blinding coldness of the snow. Lily wanted to respond to his determined cordiality, feeling that it should have sprung from her rather than from him, but there were slender contradictions about him which stirred her uneasiness and set her nerves on edge. A cigar (she thought), a good hotel, T-bone smothered in onions and whisky straight, an accomplished skirmish with the girl at the newsstand, with the girl at the telephone switchboard—all of such things would have been more in keeping than a capricious decision to pass the night in problematical comfort and certain boredom in a masked house.

"There is an excellent hotel in town, Mr. Parne. I'm thinking of your dinner; We've unfortunately few facilities for entertaining—for serving, I mean, meals."

Parne settled back in the lounge chair and sprawled his legs a little, looking Lily over: Not bad. Something like that tomato he'd put the bee on last year in Philadelphia. Very firm in all the right places and still upholstered. In fact very (to cut it short), very nice.

"Don't give it a second thought, Mrs. Elser. I'm not hard to please. I always say that potluck sometimes produces the tastiest dish. Hotels!" Lacquered fingertips brushed them away. "Your sign assured me that I wouldn't have to drive another foot. You've no idea how bad it is out and how glad I was to find shelter. What a magnificent secretary!"

Lily flushed slightly and said, "Yes, isn't it? A Sheraton."

Parne stood up and walked over to it, balancing expertly on the balls of his feet so that his movements seemed flowing. He rested fingertips on the wood's patina, softly stroking it, while his penetrating eyes flicked everything over. He *can't*, Lily told herself, walk off with that. But she knew there was nothing like that in his mind. Nothing (this conviction made it worse) so simple. A swift urgency to ask him to leave took shape, and she was trying to decide how to word it, how to *enforce* it, when Sheffield came in, looking futilely everlasting, like a pressed fern which any unaccustomed disturbance would crumble.

"The gentleman's bags are upstairs, ma'am. Would you wish me to go with you, sir, while you put your car in the garage?"

Parne turned reluctantly from the Sheraton secretary (it seemed to absorb him) and looked intently at Sheffield.

Lily said with a sharp edge of desperation, "Mr. Parne isn't staying. Mr. Parne will want dinner. He has been very kind about our lack of facilities, but I'm sure he will prefer the hotel."

Years of an ingrained and profound sense of hospitality forced Sheffield to leap into the breach before, in miserable confusion, he realized the impertinence of his move.

"We's a small roast for this evening, ma'am."

Parne's smile flashed at Lily, diligently encompassing her, broadly certain of its powers which had never (viz: tomato after tomato) let him down.

"What did I tell you, Mrs. Elser, about potluck?" The smile shifted to Sheffield. "Thank you very much. I hope the old bus will start. She's been coddled by a winter in southern California. Well, I'll be seeing you, Mrs. Elser."

Lily heard Sheffield out in the entrance hall getting things from the coat cupboard. It was like a mire where every step to extricate yourself only got you in deeper. Mr. Parne's bags were upstairs. Surely, in hotels, it must be done when any doubt existed. It would take ten minutes, possibly longer, to put the car away. She knew it stupidly vague, this expectancy, this dread that somewhere among Mr. Parne's belongings some clue would exist to focus his contradictions into an understandable explanation, no matter how melodramatic.

Like a gun (shoulder holster and harness complete—Lily knew her Class Bs) or thousands in hot money or a sealed metal case: dope. She thought, I'm the only dope. I started this tourist idea and I'll go through with it. The man's probably a traveling salesman (no, he wasn't) with a larded wife and six little larded brats all bottled in five rooms and bath in a suburb.

Lily thought this while her feet were carrying her up the wide curve of mahogany stairs. A case-hardened blonde was more likely, with a glass jaw and a speedily evanescing liver. She found Parne's bags in the end most room of the north wing. Her faint hope that they would be locked vanished. Sheffield had opened them and they gaped at Lily from a luggage stand, all bright new pigskin.

Perhaps if she just ran her fingers through their contents carefully, just felt. She did this, and everything felt like clothes except for a leather case which held toilet articles. No gun, no hot money and no dope. Nothing whatever to pin a dismissal on, to place Mr. Parne among that sinister fraternity where she felt he belonged. Faintly, from downstairs, came the sound of a closing door.

The heavy front door.

* * * *

Lorrimer Keith called at eight.

Sheffield told him while he took off his hat and coat of the advent of Mr. Parne. Sheffield regretfully feared, remembering Mr. Parne's attack upon the roast and Mr. Parne's elegant little finger movements while sipping from a glass, that Mr. Parne was not quite folks. Mr. Parne's table talk, too, had at moments been weighted with an innuendo more suitable to certain rustic odic murals than to the gentility. Colonels, of course, sometimes had a gusto for that sort of thing, but not men of the breed of Parne.

Keith's hair, had he been pelted, would have risen straight on end when he went into the living room and Lily introduced him to Parne. How like her (Keith thought, briefly gripping the white, dead-like hand) to retain her charm of social courtesy even for this porker who was paying for his food and bed.

"Wretched night, Mr. Parne."

"You've said it, Keith. I certainly thank the little lady here for having a place to hole into. Local?"

"Oh—yes, I live in town."

"What's your line?"

"Banking."

"I get it." Parne smiled jovially and patted Keith on the back. "A Republican. Well, it takes all kinds. Me, I'm in leather. I'll use your library to get off some mail if it's all right with you Mrs. Elser."

"Certainly. The stationery—"

"Take it easy. I'll find it. Glad to meet you, Keith."

They waited until Parne's wake was gone.

"Lily—"

"I know, Lorrimer, but what could we expect? It's all part of the game. I'll shower you with clichés in a minute, like taking the bitter with the sweet."

"Lily, you can't be here alone with that man."

"But I'm not."

"Oh, those two." Keith shook Sheffield and Delilah out of the picture. "Look here, I'll get hold of somebody—I'll send my housekeeper up to stay with you."

"I'd feel like a fool. No, honestly, Lorrimer, just look at it from my point of view. I've started a business venture and I'm going to run it as a businesswoman, not as a social violet. I'm not a social violet, Lorrimer. I'm tough."

"Very tough. Just the same, Mrs. Buck moves in."

"Seriously, Mrs. Buck does not. Very seriously."

"I'd sleep better. Honestly I would, Lily."

"I'm afraid it's still insomnia."

The steel, it was out again, from beneath all of her lovely softness, and Keith wondered what on earth you could do. Wondered also whether she might not be right or, conversely, whether it mightn't be better if Lily were to get a stomachful at the outset and then give the whole idea up. When you looked at it sanely there wasn't any outright *danger*. The world was filled with Parnes and they rarely, as individuals, ran amok, any more so than any other individuals. No, you really couldn't put a finger on any concrete objection, and his feeling about Parne was nothing but distaste, nothing more than plain snobbishness of the rankest sort. Yes, perhaps a good dose right at the start...

"I suppose if you insist, Lily."

"I do, Lorrimer."

He took papers from his pocket and Lily signed them, mortgaging the Benjamin West.

"I had hoped to stay for a while, Lily, but they've called some fool meeting of the Board of Trades." (To stay not only for the evening but for the night, a wakeful police dog on the stubborn alert against Parne, but that would be something. Something for Laurel Falls. Funny, a total stranger could come along and hand over a few bucks and stay all night, and not so much as a tongue-tip would wag. But if a friend who had his own home in town did it. *Lord*!) "Your balance is good and healthy again at the bank. So any time you want to quit this, Lily."

"Thanks, Lorrimer. And you know how I feel about everything you've done. Good night."

"Good night."

* * * *

It couldn't very well be Lorrimer coming back again.

Not at ten o'clock.

Lily opened wider the hall door of her bedroom. Possibly Mr. Parne had gone to the stables to get something from his car and it was he whom she had heard closing the heavy front door.

A voice called faintly from below: "Darling? Where are you?"

There was no other voice like that one, certainly not for Lily, like Nan's. The swift surge of joy which she always felt whenever Nan, un-expectedly, would be near her was pricked by a stab of fear. What on earth had brought the child home? Lily thought: I'm worrying again at shadows. I'll turn into a neurotic idiot if this keeps up. But the money Nan had wanted was concrete, and that puzzling sentence in her letter: *Things just do happen, don't they, Mother?*

Lily forced herself to put the thought with its nameless implications aside. She managed to call loudly, "Nan, dear, I'm up here. I'm coming down. I'm so *glad*, darling." She managed, too, to run down the broad curved stairs, to look with welcoming eagerness at Nan, snowflaked and bundled in mittens and furs, glowing faced, to take Nan in her arms and press her, all frosty, tightly to her. And smile.

"I had to come."

"But of course, darling."

"I lost my job."

"There—now the galoshes—do sit down, dear."

"I've used very little more out of the fifty than the bus fare, Mother. There's scads left."

"Your hands are icy. Soup or hot chocolate?"

"Hot chocolate, please, Mother. Mother—that sign at the gates. I hadn't any idea. Oh, *Mother*!"

"Stop it. It's coming down tomorrow. Lorrimer's fixing everything until the mines are worked again." (Into the discard with any more finer feelings, let Sheffield's and Delilah's ceremented recriminations fall where they might. Mortgage—sell everything: the glass, the silver, the Vanderlin, the Rembrandt Peale, the fry. Sell Sheffield and Delilah. But have no more Parnes in the house with Nan at home.) "*Stop* it, Nan, I say."

"All right."

Sheffield, looking utterly unsalable, was coming long the hall.

"Miss Nan, I do declare. I'se heard your voice. Well, welcome home."

Now that's funny, Lily thought. Nan was doing nothing about Sheffield's greeting. Nan was looking over Lily's shoulder toward the library doorway. At Parne. Lily's heart stopped dead. It was later, much later during the insufferable hours of the night, before Lily was able to dissect the one intense look that passed between Parne and Nan, like a cold clear light in darkness before a veiling mist set in. Only one thing was certain to Lily at the moment: they knew each other. Then at last Nan said, "Thank you, Sheffield. Do you think that Delilah could produce some hot chocolate?"

"I jest knows as she can, Miss Nan."

Lily felt her lips saying, "Nan, dear, this is Mr. Parne. Mr. Parne is taking one of our rooms for the night. My daughter."

"I'm pleased to meet you, Miss Elser."

"Mr. Parne."

"This is surely no night to be abroad in."

"It is pretty grim."

(They weren't looking at each other now. Just talking. Holding their eyes, with a certain care, just off each other's faces.)

"Come from far?"

"From Detroit by bus, Mr. Parne."

"Well, I bet it was tough going, although I must say those babies can pound over the road no matter what the weather is. It beats me." Then once more he looked at Nan directly. "Yes sir, it docs beat me—Miss Elser." Parne's good, strong teeth flashed brightly at Lily. "Would it be all right if some of that proposed hot chocolate was shared by the lodger?"

"Of course. Shall we go into the living room?"

* * * *

The clock struck one.

Lily turned on the reading lamp beside her bed. She realized it was useless to try to sleep. And it was then, after moments of thinking, that the look between Nan and Parne became finite: there had been recognition in it and, on Nan's part, shock. Recognition had lain in Parne's but there had been no shock, rather, after an initial touch of surprise, almost an expression of satisfaction. A satisfaction at something unexpectedly—Lily tried to segregate the proper word—helpful.

Five people in the storm-swept house. Herself and Nan here in the south wing, with Sheffield and Delilah on the floor above to the rear, and, in the north wing, Parne. It gave Lily a curious satisfaction to focus this factual picture in her mind, like a map stuck with bright-headed pins. Nan's rooms were separated from her own by the suite that had been Milton's. Lily had wanted in her deep worry to suggest to Nan that Nan spend the night with her, in the hope that during the peculiar intimacy of the close, warm darkness the years would be effected and Nan would tell her what the trouble was, as she always had when she was little, and tell her what definite fright had brought into her eyes that look of shock.

Fright—fear—the words were out now, and Lily thought she might as well face them. Nan *was* afraid, the way a young animal is afraid of something formless but which comes closer and closer with an inexorable sense of fate. It was so stupid to tell yourself that you were stupid, to upbraid yourself for what was done. It had seemed so wise to Lily to place distance between Nan and Gene Forrest. At the time. But now, even with Gene's record of past capers, with his youth, with *anything*—how much better it would be.

The clock struck two.

Three.

Lily went into the bathroom and bathed her face with cold water. She pulled a chair up close to the basin and sat for a while, wetting the cloth and pressing it across her grating eyes. It didn't help much, and she wondered just what would help. Waiting wouldn't. Just waiting never had. Attack? Go straight to Parne and clear this fog and find out precisely where the field of battle lay? Go and face him and tell him that she knew that he and Nan knew each other, and she knew that he had come to the house purposely (but she didn't, not *know* it, but she had to) and what was there between them?

Five o'clock struck as Lily let herself out into the hall.

She had taken several steps before the darkness struck her like a blow, making this house which was her own seem unfamiliar, for she had never moved about in it before without lights. She went more swiftly through this inimical strangeness, to the left, past the wide vault of the stairway, to the left again and then on until her fingers brushed Parne's door. Any hesitation would have defeated her, so she rapped lightly, waited and then rapped again.

"Mr. Parne?"

There was, Lily realized, small need for any whispering. She doubted whether even a scream could be heard by Nan or Sheffield or Delilah in their distant places in the house. She rapped more loudly and said more loudly, "Mr. Parne!"

A revulsion of fear overcame her as she recalled her earlier pictures of a stranger wandering through the rooms, moving with stealthily investigating footsteps along the halls. Suppose Parne were behind her, standing perfectly still and listening and watching and making up his mind just what he was going to do. Her fingers closed on the knob in panic and she opened the door.

She said into what was still just further darkness, "Mr. Parne—I—This is Mrs. Elser, Mr. Parne!"

He must be gone, because she caught no sound of breathing. If he wasn't just lying there quietly and holding his breath. Lily found the switch for the ceiling lights and pressed it.

Parne grinned at her from the floor.

He was dead. Lily stood there without effort, feeling no weight on her feet, while she thought of the Latin for that grin which at times twists the lips of the dead. Risor—risum—mortis—and all the while she floated on air over closer to Parne. Otherwise (ignoring the grin) he was so neat.

Saffron silk pajamas were open at the throat, exposing a V of thick black hair shaved across the top in a straight hard line. Leather slippers were on his feet and a roman-striped linen bathrobe over his pajamas. His head was across the sill of the bathroom doorway, his leather slippers toward her.

Then, thoughtfully, his tongue stuck out.

* * * *

Light was a faint gray against windows when Lily came to with Parne beside her, dead on the floor. She felt stronger and far more sane. She got to her feet and looked at Parne's wrist watch on the bedtable. Six o'clock. Sheffield and Delilah would be waking up, then getting up, then coming downstairs and very soon finding that Mr. Parne was a corpse.

Shot.

Blood on the bathrobe told Lily that. The gun told her that. It lay just inside the hall doorway. She recognized it as the small pearl-handled .22 which Milton had kept in the drawer of the secretary down in the living room. The Sheraton. It had to be that gun. Pearl handles were so rare that they scarcely existed any more. Lily had known it was kept in the secretary; Nan had known, and Nan had known Parne and Parne had known Nan—a second surge of faintness forced Lily to sit down before she would fall down.

She desperately wanted advice. Lorrimer Keith could advise her; so could Dr. Colin Starr, who had attended Milton during his final illness. Gene Forrest could. But none of them could. Because she would have to say: A man has been murdered, shot by a gun that we kept in the secretary in the living room, and Nan knew him. Never (this at least was clear and final) must anyone ever know that Nan knew him.

The letters.

The letters which Parne had gone into the library to write. There might be references, something in them to establish a connection between himself and Nan. Lily fought back her faintness and stood up. Ten terribly careful minutes satisfied her that there were no letters in Parne's clothing or in the room. Unless they were in the open bags on the luggage stand.

Sheffield and Delilah would by now be out of bed.

Lily went over to the bags. This time she didn't just run her fingers through them. She took everything out. That, of course, was why she had missed it before: flat on the bottom of the Gladstone. Staring straight up at her. It was a picture. A cabinet photograph of Nan.

She took it out of the bag, thinking: Well, it's true. No chance had brought Parne to the house. That, naturally, was final. His coddled car in southern California, his heading East, his avid relief at the signboard which had spared him further storm-harried steps, all of those fictions could be jettisoned with assurety. What had there been, what *could* there have been between a man like Parne and a girl like Nan to (yes, face it!) have driven Nan into taking the little pearl-handled gun and—

Sheffield and Delilah would be pretty well dressed.

Then something about the portrait held her. It wasn't Nan at nineteen, at now. For more than a year Nan had been wearing her hair fairly short with a careful youthful carelessness that had satisfied, apparently, Nan's nascent spirit of revolt—whatever it had done to her appearance. The hair was up in the picture, far off the face, in the fashion of a couple of years back when hats had stayed on only after hours of tactful effort and collusions. And the hair seemed longer.

The mat was embossed with the Detroit branch crest of Endermann & Endermann.

Two years ago Nan *had* been away for six weeks during the summer, taking a course in design in Cleveland, living there at the Young Women's Christian Association, working daily at the Elkhart studios which were run by that violent Austrian woman who had never got over batiks. In Cleveland, not in Detroit. Not, however, so very far away from Detroit.

…and had shot Mr. Parne.

Delilah would be putting their bed in order, and Sheffield would be ending the intricate knotting of his tie.

Nan on the witness stand. The polite district attorney. The motive. The sudden tough district attorney. The motive. There must be no murder.

No. Mr. Parne was not murdered. Mr. Parne committed suicide. The gun would have to be put closer. It would have to be put into Mr. Parne's dead hand. Lily picked the gun up and wiped it with her negligee. That wasn't enough.

Doorknobs.

Mr. Parne dragged easily: a loose, fluid weight. His slippers came off, showing nicely tended feet. Must remember to put them back on. Lily wiped the knobs of the hall door, letting Mr. Parne lie on the floor. Then she pressed his right, complacent hand on both knobs. She pulled him back again so that his head once more lay across the sill of the bathroom doorway, because there was some blood on the floor and he ought to be beside it as he had been. She tore the cabinet photograph into small pieces and flushed them down in the bathroom. She put the slippers back on Parne's nice feet. The gun looked all right in his hand, even though his fingers were indifferent about gripping it.

Lily backed away from the bathroom doorway, hysterically fascinated by Mr. Parne's broad grin.

* * * *

It was her room.

It was her bed.

The clock struck eight.

Lily roused, under the slight shaking of her arm, from the warm, blessed confusion of exhausted sleep into which her breaking nerves had plunged her.

"Oh—good morning, Delilah. What time is it?"

"Good mawning, madam. It is eight."

The full force of recollection pierced Lily. Somehow, instantly, she must warn Nan—no, not warn, but must be constantly near her, strongly close to her, to say clearly, firmly: Suicide. When the body was found.

"I thought you had better know, madam."

(Here it was.)

"Yes, Delilah?"

"We just got us another tourist. He's a pleasant-spoken gentleman from Kansas City, Kans., and he's gone got himself all tuckered out from fighting that there blizzard through the night."

"No—Delilah, we can't—I mean I've arranged things at the bank. The sign is coming down."

"Wish I'd known of that, madam. I reckon it's too late. As I done said, he was a dead-tired gentleman so I showed him straight up to the room next to Mr. Parne's. He said he planned on just to take a good hot tub and then turn in. I done explained to him, madam, about the bathroom being in between."

CHAPTER 2

How do you dress for the death of a stranger?

Lily amended this into how do you dress for the death of a stranger when you (still) don't know about it. She kept her eyes just past Delilah's face, which had acquired with the years the texture of a placid coconut, and thought: Every hour from now on I must be on guard against mistakes such as that. They are the little signposts which lead the mind trained in criminology into unmasking you. A minute-by-minute vigilance against the fatality of minor slips. I know nothing Mr. Parne is—was—a stranger who applied for lodgings out of the storm. At eleven o'clock last night he said good night to my daughter and to myself and went to bed.

"Have you the gentleman's name, Delilah?"

"Yes, madam. Mr. Horace Hangaway from Kansas City, Kans. Maybe it's jest because he's so tuckered, but he's a mighty peaked-looking gentleman. His eyes appears like they been all burned up."

"He—how long has he been here?"

"Why, he's jest come, madam. Sheffield is putting his car away because he was too far wore-out to do it by hisself. Will I take breakfast up to Mr. Parne or do I wait until he rings?"

Lily's hand did not quiver on the counterpane but lay there placidly, almost (she thought) as though it really belonged to her.

"I would wait, Delilah, until Mr. Parne rings."

"Yes, madam. May I draw your bath?"

"Please. And the gray wool, Delilah."

"Yes, madam."

It was important to be dressed, to feel the bulwark of clothes about you when the climax would be faced. You could not dress in seconds, not bathe and dress, not with casual normality, and surely seconds were all that would be granted. If even they. If only Delilah for once wouldn't putter, be deliberate about bath temperatures; would simply turn on water, then rip the gray wool from the closet and then go.

The sound of water peacefully pouring came from the bathroom, then it was stronger, and finally it steadied down. Perhaps Mr. Horace Hangaway of Kansas City, Kans., had not been able to take it any more than Lily had: the neatness of Mr. Parne and the impersonal quality of his sticking tongue. Mr. Hangaway with his general peakedness and his clinker eyes might have fainted too.

Knuckles rapped briefly on the hall door.

"Delilah!"

"Yes, madam?"

"See who that is, please."

"It's me, Mother," Nan's voice called through the panels.

"Darling—come in."

She looked like a schoolgirl across the room through the muffled light which the storm gave with its still-falling snow, until she got close to you, and then it was obvious to Lily that Nan hadn't slept, and Lily thought: She *isn't* a child any longer; she's getting the woman look.

"Did you sleep well, dear?"

"Yes, Mother. And you?"

"Perfectly."

Delilah was satisfied about the bath. She was laying the gray wool on a chaise-longue, removing its hanger, smoothing its folds.

"The dark oxfords, madam?"

"Please, Delilah."

Go—go—go—but no, now don't go, don't leave me alone with Nan, with this girl stranger who must be waiting just as I am waiting, with a wall of glass between us.

"Shall we breakfast in here, Mother?"

"I think not, dear." (Just as with clothing, the defensive properties of one of the public rooms would be safer for the blow.) "There's the extra work, with Mr. Hangaway, with Mr. Parne."

"I'se can manage, madam."

"We will breakfast downstairs, Delilah."

"Yes, madam."

Delilah went, leaving Nan standing close over by a window with her back turned and with nobody knew what expression of despairing bleakness in her eyes which studied, presumably, the falling snow. Lily slipped on a robe and started calmly toward the bathroom.

"I shan't be a moment, dear."

"All right, Mother. Is there, is there somebody else?"

"Yes. A Mr. Hangaway came this morning. Delilah didn't know— that the sign was coming down, I mean. She arranged for him to stay." Irresistibly Lily went over to Nan and took her in her arms and kissed her, because she had to feel her and somehow recapture the very fact of their relationship to one another, but the wall was still there, even though her arms went through it. "Don't worry, darling."

"Of course not, Mother." Then Nan did turn sharply. Her face was still in shadow because of the snow glow behind it. "Worry?"

Lily said swiftly, "About the tourist problem, dear," and went into the bathroom and closed its door.

Lily used no soap, nothing, none of the pleasant array of accessories which Milton had always wanted her to have for leisurely, scented bathing. Just into the water and out, and a rapid drying. There was something wrong, from the very fact that the blow had *not* fallen before now. Mr. Hangaway's door to the bathroom might have been bolted on the inside, of course, by Mr. Parne, and Mr. Hangaway might be waiting until his neighbor would be through; might even, in his exhaustion, have decided to skip the proposed hot tub and have tumbled his peaked and tuckered-out body straight into bed. That would be worse, as the waiting would be prolonged.

Only the gray wool now and the oxfords.

"Nan, darling."

"Mother?"

"Gene Forrest was here. He called yesterday afternoon."

"Yes?"

"Lorrimer Keith seems to think rather well of him, about his prospects. He thinks Gene has steadied."

"Oh."

"Yes. Gene noticed the tourist sign in passing. It upset him. He felt the vocal touch about it, the baying of the wolves." (Keep talking, just talking.) "I reassured him, I hope, that we were still divorced from imminent starvation, and I also felt rather as if I'd underestimated him. I liked him yesterday very much. Well, shall we go down? Popovers, I think, and eggs? Bacon?"

Mr. Hangaway was seated on the lowest step of the broad curved stairway: a gaunt, dark bundle in the hall's uncertain twilight. He was wearing a stained woolen bathrobe from which his wrists and shins stuck out, pipe-like. His neck was pipe-like, too, and seemed far too reedy for his bony, large head which possessed the merest minimum of flesh. He made no move to get out of their way as Lily, followed by Nan, neared him but sat on, a lonely bundle of spindles, in some remote world of his own.

Lily said quickly, "Go back upstairs, darling. Delilah told me that Mr. Hangaway was—warn out."

Hangaway's voice was frightening because of its strength. You were unprepared for such power from that skeleton source. He did not bother to look around.

"I'm not worn out. I'm sick. There's a dead man in the bathroom. Go and take a look if you don't believe me. He shot himself."

Lily's arm was around Nan, pressing her cruelly close and tight. The cue had come so smoothly, with such profound relief.

"Suicide?"

"Yes. The gun is in his hand. His head is over the sill and I might have stepped on it. God, but I am sick!" Hangaway's head dipped forward until it swung between his knees, a large ripe melon on the thinnest of stems. "Get me a doctor, please. And maybe you'd better do something about the police."

"A doctor, of course—Doctor Starr—possibly, I mean it's so difficult to be certain about death—"

"Don't worry about that. He's dead all right. Like mutton."

* * * *

Dr. Colin Starr viewed the morning with distaste. The blizzard had not died with the night, and outdoor movements would be on a level, he supposed, with the popularized version of Balto's dash (plus serum) to a stricken Nome. A prospect which gave him no pleasure. He stoked up heavily on rashers of bacon, on eggs, having because of his build plenty of bunker space. The early forties became him.

Starr sometimes reflected on the sharper brilliancies of the larger world, of the greater centers, the more rapid tempos of nationally famous minds, and always decided his own puddle to be preferable. His large fine house which his grandfather had built in the solidest tradition of mansard roofs, with its garden and its lawn that faced on Onega Drive, satisfied him completely as a good shelter and a good place for his work.

Starr's secretary, Miss Wadsworth, came hurriedly into the dining room, looking very upset in her frame of stiff white starches.

"Mrs. Elser has just phoned, Doctor. A man, a tourist, she thinks he is dead. She thinks that he shot himself. Mrs. Elser had decided on taking in tourists, but not any longer. I mean now that *this* has happened. Oh, I am so sorry for her."

"Yes, of course. I never realized things were so bad."

No (while Starr drove his car through the storm), he had not realized that Milton Elser must have left his affairs in such a state. He could not picture Lily Elser as a hostess for uncertain strays. She lacked the metal which such a job required. This suicide business was pretty shocking, especially if the man were dead. Even if he weren't it was bad enough, even if the man were to pull through. Starr damned the drifts, the ruts, the blinding snow and this dark, vague pall of the ceaseless storm.

An hour after he had reached the house and after he had finished his business with Parne's body Starr sat with Lily in the living room downstairs. Lily decided that this was going to be tough, worse than the police had been and District Attorney Heffernan, during their brief and polite initial questioning of her when they had arrived.

Lily liked and admired Starr very much because he was solid and kind, and although he, too, had that protective look it was a comfortably general one which encompassed humanity as a lump and not just specifically her. But he knew you so well. No matter what your lips or your face might be saying Lily felt he knew what you were really saying on the inside to yourself.

She appreciated the futility of trying to deceive him. She wouldn't think of trying it if it were just for her own sake, but nothing, not even his peculiar powers for sensing the truth in you, was going to prevent her from trying because of Nan.

"I'm terribly sorry that all this should have happened, Mrs. Elser."

"Was there nothing could be done?"

"Done? Oh no. He died several hours before I got here, somewhere in the neighborhood of four or five o'clock." (Lily bit her lips sharply to prevent diem from saying: At five, Doctor, because of the tongue.) "We're arranging to get Mr. Hangaway out of here shortly."

Lily didn't care about that. She cared nothing about Mr. Hangaway and his inability to stomach the shock of a look on sudden death. It was of Parne that she wanted to hear: what Starr thought, what the police thought, if they were satisfied that Parne had taken his own life.

"Was Mr. Hangaway so seriously shocked, Doctor?"

"No, it isn't shock. I've sent for male attendants and the ambulance. He'll be taken to the hospital."

"Male attendants?"

"Yes. It's all right for you to know now that the danger is over. The man is an addict. The morphine and syringe, the usual paraphernalia, they were in his bag. You've had a lucky escape, Mrs. Elser. You and your daughter."

"He might have been dangerous?"

"Very dangerous. You never know how a man of that type is going to jump." Starr smiled at Lily reassuringly, brushing aside with a vague gesture the appalling shock it had been to him when he had realized that Hangaway might have passed a night in the secluded loneliness of the house with Lily Elser and her daughter and with nothing to deter him but the moth-like fragility of two old Negro servants. He kept carefully from showing in his eyes his case-history knowledge of what addicts like Hangaway had done: the sex crimes with their insensate brutality, the lust for instigating and then fanning pain into a tortured death. "Just when did Mr. Hangaway reach here, Mrs. Elser?"

"Shortly before eight."

"Yes, so Delilah told us. We were interested in having you confirm it."

"I know it was then, because Delilah woke me at eight and told me he had just come." (This was leading up to something. You could tell that. Above the still-untasted horror of Mr. Hangaway being an addict there were arrows that pointed toward Parne.) "He told Delilah that he had been driving all night and that he felt worn out."

"The district attorney was rather hoping he'd come here sooner."

"Mr. Heffernan? Wondered—why?"

"Yes. He wondered whether there might not have been some connection between the two men under the circumstances."

This was it all right. You didn't say a thing like "under the circumstances" if things were smooth and unquestioned and slotted in their grooves.

"Does Mr. Heffernan feel that Mr. Hangaway could have been responsible for Mr. Parne's suicide?" (A stereotyped plot pattern presented itself and Lily seized it.) "Something of a nemesis, Doctor? Mr. Parne felt that Mr. Hangaway was catching up with him and killed himself rather than face—whatever it was he had to face?"

"No, Mrs. Elser. I hate putting this on you all at once. Mr. Parne was killed. He was shot in the back, just below the left shoulder blade. I imagine from some distance. The bullet didn't come out."

Lily shut her eyes for one moment while the betraying weakness swept through her. All of her feverish gestures in the night in that room, born of her sickness and terror, had been a waste and a mocking futility: the fingerprints on the doorknobs and the gun, all of that dragging and lugging of Parne with the feel of his loose, loose limbs away from and then back again to the blood on the floor. Why hadn't she thought of examining the wound?

Then the concern split into her that the negligee which she had worn while going into Parne's room was red. Red upon its redness there might well be a spot of blood. Upon something of Nan's, whatever it was that Nan had worn on her own desperate mission, some touch of the damning carmine might be too.

"It is so incredible, Doctor. It makes me doubt fact. No one was here last night but Mr. Parne and ourselves."

"Yes, we know. It's what bothers them. It's why Heffernan is still hoping that some connection may turn up with Hangaway. It would be so logical if it would, because an addict of Hangaway's nature wouldn't have the slightest scruple about killing, no matter how tenuous the motive. Heffernan feels it too coincidental for credence that a potential killer, such as Hangaway, should turn up here just by chance on the heels of a homicide."

"Can't they make him talk, Doctor?" (How useless, Lily reflected, this eagerness which she pressed into her voice. Mr. Hangaway could talk his head off, and nothing would efface her withering knowledge of a link between Mr. Parne and Nan, of the fright in Nan's eyes, of Nan's picture and of Milton's own little pearl-handled gun.) "Can't they find anything in his papers, his things?"

"No, there's nothing of any value to the police in his papers, and he won't be able to talk for some time. He had started to get pretty violent. I gave him an injection. Mrs. Elser, these are just the abominable situations which sometimes we have to go through. We'll take Hangaway off very shortly, and they're arranging about Mr. Parne. Within an hour or so your house will be your own again."

A flood of unbelievable relief went through Lily.

"Do you mean that Nan and I—we could go away?"

Starr looked at her curiously. There was something there. Something deeper, of a more violent urgency than a simple desire to leave a house where tragedy had occurred.

"I'm afraid I couldn't say. That possibility isn't within my province, Mrs. Elser."

"No, I appreciate that, Doctor. When anyone meets death suddenly—"

Starr said earnestly, "You've nothing on earth to worry about." He felt, after he said it, that his attempt at lightening the situation fell far short from being effective. "Neither you nor your daughter is the type to shoot a stranger. I can assure you that the thought hasn't even been considered, and that Heffernan, that everyone has nothing but sympathy for you and will get you through the necessary steps as simply as they can."

"Just what are the necessary steps, Doctor?"

"They're entirely un-alarming. They're looking for signs of forcible entry by the killer during the night. They'll trace the gun. They'll make an exhaustive search of the house and outbuildings and grounds. Then they won't bother you here any more. They'll concentrate on checking Parne's past."

Lily's slender fingers tightened lightly.

"Do you know how they do that, Doctor?"

"I don't exactly, but they've astonishing facilities for it. However, that's nothing for you to worry about. The only other thing they'll want you to stay around for will be the inquest."

"They can't—they won't want Nan at that?"

"Perhaps it could be arranged but, frankly, I doubt it. She did meet Parne last night and talk with him. They're likely to insist on having all the firsthand evidence about the man they can get." (Starr thought:

Here's a woman who is badly in need of help. Why on earth doesn't she loosen up and tell me what's really worrying her? It's beyond money trouble; it's beyond Parne. There's something feral about it, a guarded tigress touch. Good lord, perhaps it's there: her young.) "About her, Mrs. Elser—about your daughter."

"Yes, Doctor?"

"I know how this has upset her, but beyond that. It struck me when I talked with her that things weren't quiet right. As if there were something on her mind."

"Well"—Lily managed to smile—"she did lose her job."

"In Detroit, wasn't it?"

"Yes, Nan has been doing free-lance fashion designing. I suppose there was the new broom angle about it, in that her start was such a success. She won a competition which the *Detroit Free Press* conducted. It gave her a good deal of publicity and brought her in quite a lot of orders. She even had her picture"—the bright smile on Lily's face froze into a grimace—"in the papers, Doctor."

Starr smiled back at Lily while appreciating the grimace and while wishing he could shake her into being sensible and into getting this incubus off her mind. It was not necessary for him to remind himself that most of his women patients went through initial periods of stubbornness which would have sated a mule.

"Then I suppose," he said, "that people just stopped being fashionable?"

"Something like that, Doctor."

"Well, she'll get over it. The young do. At least she's at home again, and that's something for all of her friends here to be thankful for. Will both of you dine with me tonight, Mrs. Elser?" (Gene Forrest—Lorrimer Keith—Gene's mother—the Tomlinson kids—they could be rounded up.) "Some of your daughter's friends are coming. I'm sure you'll both sleep better after a change of—well—scene."

Quite suddenly Lily started to cry. Not much, but she knew it would be the beginning of a good case of hysterics if she didn't instantly stop it. Goodness, kindness, they were the things she couldn't stand up against right now. They turned her strength into water.

"This is stupid of me, Doctor. We'll be glad to."

Starr stood up and held out his hand. He ignored her tears entirely.

"Then at eight?"

"At eight."

* * * *

They removed Mr. Hangaway at eleven.

It took two burly attendants from the psychopathic ward to do so, and even they failed to muffle his strong voice with its initial outpouring of obscenities when they started to force him down the broad curved stairs. Lily heard them, sitting in her private living room with Nan, and talked calmly through them.

Mr. Hangaway was out. Out of their lives forever. Which left simply Mr. Parne. Just herself and Nan and Mr. Parne's murdered body in between them. It and the wall of glass which Lily insisted on keeping there, because she knew that the moment she let into her full consciousness the first concrete shape, the first absolute fact, she would no longer be a strong protector but would go to pieces. Nothing but complete ignorance of truth could be her safeguard and her armor.

Sheffield knocked and came in, and said that District Attorney Heffernan would be pleased if Mrs. Elser would consent to join him downstairs in the living room.

"I'll be back shortly, Nan dear. We'll lunch up here. Something simple, Sheffield. Tell Delilah that sandwiches will do and tea."

"Yes ma'am."

"You might ask her to have some ready for the gentlemen of the police. If they are still here."

"Yes ma'am."

Lily had met District Attorney Heffernan casually at various affairs at the country club, occasionally at the houses of mutual friends. She thought him a pleasant man, one normally tinged with a preoccupation in his work, and knew that officially his terms in office (he had served two) had been highly satisfactory to the town.

He turned from a contemplation of the still-curtaining snowfall and came over to greet her, taking her hand and smiling with, it seemed to Lily, an unusual air of formality. She thought: I'm sensitive to shadings right now. I must keep things in their true proportions.

"I must thank you, Mr. Heffernan, you and Doctor Starr, for arranging about Mr. Hangaway."

"I suppose the doctor told you how lucky you were. What an escape!"

"Yes. Won't you sit down?"

"Thank you." Heffernan smiled briefly, almost boyishly, in fleeting concession to his hearty liking of Lily Elser and of everything he'd ever heard about her. "I'm sorry you find me in the second of my personalities. My official one."

"Naturally, Mr. Heffernan. In fact, you find me in mine. A dispenser of lodgings. It turned out a rather disastrous one. I'm doing it no longer."

"I should hope not. I can't understand how Lorrimer Keith ever let you."

"He did try to dissuade me. I put my foot down."

Here was the trouble, Heffernan reflected, with dual personalities: You had to goad into action the one which you knew became you least.

"I don't suppose you noticed the gun, Mrs. Elser? The one that was in Parne's hand?"

"No, not really. I did see a gun there, and then Mr. Hangaway had spoken about it when he told us that he had found Mr. Parne."

"Well, the gun was one of Mr. Elser's. The case for it was in that secretary over there."

"Milton's? He had one, of course—but, of *course*, Mr. Heffernan. I remember it now."

"Yes, Mrs. Elser?"

"Mr. Parne had scarcely been here more than five or ten minutes when he noticed that secretary, because it's a Sheraton. I remember he went over to it and examined it quite carefully. In fact," (yes, thank God, Sheffield *had* been here) "Sheffield came into the room while he was doing so and asked Mr. Parne about putting away his car."

"Good. That does help a little. You've no idea how hard it is to get things clear. Did Parne strike you as a man who would be especially interested in antiques?"

"Frankly he didn't. But he did recognize that the secretary was good."

"We'll naturally know more about that angle when we know more about Parne." Heffernan's gray, solid eyes turned toward the windows. "Our blizzard is a quiet one, Mrs. Elser. No howling winds. It has a muffling quality about it. Did you hear anything, any unusual sound whatever in the house during the night?"

"No, none at all."

"It's a curious situation. We know that somebody must have come into the house, but we don't know how. They have a good man on the force for this forcible-entry business, and he's decided that there's nothing doing. Whoever killed Parne must have been let in through one of the doors. Let in by someone already here."

"But that's impossible."

"No, we think that possibly Parne let the man in himself." He could not look directly at her. "We've *got* to think that, Mrs. Elser."

Lily said equably—she hoped so fervently that her voice did sound equable—"But why would he?"

"We don't know. It would presuppose a rendezvous, wouldn't you think? I can't see Parne coming downstairs and letting in a stranger.

Possibly Parne went outside the house and met him at some appointed spot in town, but I can't figure him then bringing the man back here. No, we've got to presuppose that Parne came to this house not through any chance, not as a passing tourist, but intentionally, and that his killer knew Parne was going to do so."

"I can think of no reason on earth why Mr. Parne should have come here."

"No more can we. And still, any other supposition seems to make less sense if we want to connect the two men, Parne and Hangaway. Then there must be a motive. Every murder has a motive, Mrs. Elser, even for a dope fiend like Hangaway. Our chief difficulty is that the motive probably lies in the past, and we don't know Parne's past. We don't, so far, know a thing about him. You've not remembered anything further that he said last night, Mrs. Elser?"

"No, he spoke of the west coast, that he was driving East. That's all, beyond the most general sort of conversation."

"Well"—Heffernan looked at Lily for one penetrating instant and then stood up, smiling his smile and holding out his hand—"thanks for helping us about the gun. We can think of Parne as finding it himself in the secretary. That will do for a starter. Perhaps of his coming downstairs after you and Miss Elser had gone to bed and looking at the secretary again. This time looking through it and finding the gun. Then either meeting his killer outside and bringing him back here or just letting him in. Then the killer took the gun away from Parne and shot him and fixed things up to look like a suicide. I'm afraid that it couldn't be thinner, but any picture does for a beginning. Doctor Starr tells me that you and Miss Elser are dining with him tonight?"

"Yes. He thought the change of scene—"

"And a very sound thought. Incidentally we feel that you may be nervous for a night or two. It wouldn't be natural if you weren't. I've persuaded the chief to have a man stay here nights. You and your daughter will feel more secure. He won't be a bother but will just sit out in the hallway—if that will be agreeable to you, Mrs. Elser?"

"Quite." Lily forced the smile on again, thinking that by now it must be pretty threadbare. "It's good of you, very kind of you to think of it, Mr. Heffernan."

* * * *

Mr. Parne, in a basket, left at three.

Lily's eyes were leaden. It seemed to her that she had never slept. The brief hour and a half that she had caught last night in her exhaustion were nothing. Wave after wave of wanting to sleep flowed through her, dragging down her eyelids and drugging any coherence in her thoughts. If she could rest some, really rest for several hours, then she felt that she could handle things as they came along.

She took the red velvet negligee from its hanger and went with it over to a window. Blood, she instructed her drugged intelligence, did not stay red. It dried out something darker: a brown. She saw nothing on the short soft pile, but after her tired, hot eyes had begun to glaze with red her fingers found a patch of stiffness. Naturally blood would harden and get stiff. Stupid not to have thought of that. It was there all right: quite a patch of it, under the right sleeve, which was cut very full and flowing, where her arm had encircled Mr. Parne's deadweight looseness while she had been pressing his willing hand upon the doorknobs. Well, water got out blood.

Lily filled the washbasin in the bathroom with the lukewarm water (hot either set blood or didn't; cold, ditto) and let the right sleeve of the negligee sink in it and soak. Casually the water grew pink and then pinker, a pink that meant but one thing to Lily: Mr. Parne. He was materializing before her vague eyes like a print in a tray of developer. Neatly, just as he had been neat.

She would have to put her fingers into the water and stir Mr. Parne up to get rid of the last drop of him. Then rinse and rinse and rinse. Well, she couldn't.

Lily stood for a while just pressing her hands down flat on the cold white marble and wanting to go to sleep. It would be so sensible to go to sleep and just permit the sleeve to float there and soak, then to wake up and find the last trace of the man gone. Joining himself in his basket.

She had no idea for how long Nan had been standing behind her in the bathroom doorway. Time was an element of such inconsequential relativity that Lily for once, and never again, enjoyed a thorough comprehension of the theories of Einstein. Then the red in the water and Nan made sharp sudden sense, and almost with a reflex action Lily's fingers reached swiftly and opened the drain, while her whole being jumped wide-awake. Her fingers, regardless of repulsion, sank into the tepid water, lifted velvet folds, freeing the drain, and hastened the exit of pink, which sank and gurgled and at long last vanished in a minor wail. Lily turned quietly, said quietly, "Darling, I thought you were going to rest."

"I couldn't, Mother."

The child's lips were positively stiff. She couldn't help but have seen the pink water from the doorway, not being blind.

"I'm always being disillusioned, Nan, dear."

"What, Mother?"

"This wretched stuff is supposed to be fast. It appears to run."

"I think it's supposed to be dry-cleaned only."

"I realize that now, and I hope to live long enough to learn that there's nothing so expensive as a petty economy."

"There was—something on the sleeve, Mother?"

"Tea."

Lilly squeezed the soft velvet in her hands, squeezing tighter and tighter because it was easier to do so than to treat the blood of Mr. Parne with any repellent delicacy.

"Mother."

"Nan, dear?"

"Do you know something?"

"Honestly, darling, the older I grow the more I believe I don't. This notion that wisdom comes with age is nothing but a solace for wrinkles and double chins."

"Oh, this is just it. Just as it's always been."

"What is, dear?"

"We're never close. We've never been close. Can't parents and children *ever* be close, Mother?"

The negligee dropped in moist folds to the bathroom floor. No, Lily reflected, they couldn't be. She hadn't been with her parents, and she hadn't been with her own child. Not truly so. Not in the sense of being vibrantly inside of one another in the way that it happened at rare times within two people of a similar generation, in rare marriages, with rare friends.

Love and respect, even a fine companionability, all of the sane, decent, nicer bonds could be there, but Nan was right: never could there be any honest closeness; just two loving images which strove throughout life to live up to the best of what each thought the other saw in each. Well, here was a moment for breaking a rule like that. Letting everything tumble and taking Nan in her arms and opening every bit of herself to that cry from Nan's heart.

Lily held out her hands.

She had a feeling that death was striking her right on the spot when she saw the tightness of Nan's lips draw tighter and Nan's eyes glance swiftly at and away from the hands which were wet and still dripping a little from their rinse in pink.

"I guess I will rest, Mother."

Lily watched Nan back a step or two (not turn), then walk (not run) across the living room and out into the hall. It was extraordinary what swiftness could exist in a complete about-face. Of one's mental attitude toward a thing, and one's interpretation of it. That was the bother with being so dead tired. Clearly now Lily saw Nan running outside there in the hall to her rooms. Saw Nan grabbing up whatever it was Nan had been wearing last night on her terrible mission. Letting water into her washroom basin and (again) draining out some more of Mr. Parne.

Lily picked up the negligee and went to a boxed-in radiator, spreading out the wet right sleeve, smoothing it to dry evenly over the heat. That was when she noticed the piece that had been clipped out of it, about the size of a quarter, from about the center of about where the center of the blood patch had been.

That will be (Lily thought) the state's Exhibit "A."

* * * *

Lorrimer Keith left his house at twenty past seven. Normally it was only a ten-minute drive to Lily's, but the drifts and the ruts and the falling snow would slow him up tremendously. His car was a coupe, conservative, expensive and black.

Lorrimer closed a beaver collar more warmly about his throat, tightened fur-lined gloves and reflected dreamily on all the worth of a comfortable solidity. Surely, in face of this horrible business of last night, the wretched, cruel shock of it, Lily would defy the conventions (just as he was prepared to defy them) and let him take care of herself and Nan. Let him bring them both within his shelter, no matter how few the months were that Elser had been in his grave.

They could marry quietly and go away. Rio de Janeiro was enchanting at this season of the year. Quietly (but not too quietly) in its warm, Latin gaiety Lily could bloom and Nan could have a good time. Then, after several months of colorful lassitude (parrots, maxixes, jalousies, exotic flowers, the Belasco harbor) they would come back to Laurel Falls and settle down to a vista spread with fallow fields of a peaceful domesticity. It never occurred to him for an instant but that Lily would agree to all this, because that was the way you felt about Lily.

The good-looking, uniformed young cop in the hall was something of a shock. You couldn't escape the youngster's presence, his personality, and still he seemed to flatten into a backdrop of the scene: there and yet not of it. A bright red bulb of danger, bare and unshaded, in the toned glows of this lovely house.

Lily and Nan were ready, waiting, cloaked and with galoshes on, in the living room. They came out and joined Keith immediately.

"You were an angel, Lorrimer, to have thought of coming for us."

"Of course I'm an angel, Lily. Hello, Nan."

"Hello, Mr. Keith."

(*That* would all stop pretty soon. He'd be "Lorrimer" to her in practically no time at all. Nice to have such a fine daughter all fully grown.)

"Still storming?"

"Lily, this snowfall is going down in history. Like that midget affair they're still boasting about in New York."

They heard, as they chatted in the warm richness of the coupe, the staccato explosions of a motorcycle behind them. It became impossible to ignore them.

"Glad the boys are taking such good care of you, Lily."

"Mr. Heffernan was sweet about it. Have you heard about our dope-fiend lodger?"

"Ladies, I have heard everything. Our local sheets are plastered with hot details to the point of indigestion. I've read every one of them. If Heffernan hadn't posted guards at your house I'd have got out Betsy and camped there myself."

"I thought it was Roscoe."

"And they say guns are sexless!"

"Crowding you, Nan, dear?"

"No, Mother."

"I suppose Doctor Starr won't mind if we leave early. After all, after last night."

"I imagine he'll force you to, Lily."

Lily looked young in beige chiffon and Nan very young in white organdy. Mrs. Forrest, Gene's mother, was not so successful in plum velvet, and Alice Tomlinson (Harry's twin) needed nothing but a wire hook and a Christmas tree for her candy-striped taffeta. It was all very gay.

It was (Lily thought) determinedly so: murder, addicts, the patient, watchful eyes of the law, were deliberately suffocated beneath a wealth of social pleasantries in this handsome, turn-of-the-century drawing room of Dr. Starr's.

Starr said to Lily over martinis, "I know you must be interested, so I'm bringing it up. It's about that man Hangaway."

A Capehart was softly full with a bright thing of Cole Porter's, and Lily smiled, and said, "Yes, Doctor?"

"He got back to normal during the afternoon. He's still in the hospital and under observation, of course. Heffernan has tried his best to get something out of him, but he's turned sullen. He just refuses to talk. That is, about anything that counts."

"About a possible connection with Mr. Parne?"

"Yes. His story is one of those simple tales which seem infernally impossible to check up on from a police point of view. Nobody can be pinned down to an hour-by-hour accounting of what he was doing while driving through a blizzard. Hangaway says that he started out around seven o'clock last night from Detroit."

"Detroit!" (Nan—the same vague finger of murk, of unnamable dread, its tip in Detroit, as the picture of Nan among Mr. Parne's belongings had been taken in Detroit—what was it?—*what was it* that linked her child with a Parne, with [now] an addict—the vicious center lying in Detroit?) "But I thought Mr. Hangaway came from Kansas City, which—as Delilah insists—is in Kansas?"

"He docs. But he stayed over yesterday in Detroit and didn't start out until evening. That would have made the driving time to here all right with the road conditions what they were. He says he's a free-lance writer and eventually expect to put Sinclair Lewis out of business."

"Mr. Hangaway certainly is a dope fiend."

"Oh, that part is real enough, and he does have his amusing points. Addicts can. It's one of their main dangers. They lull you with their pleasantries into a false security before, well, the other side of them comes out."

"He says he only stayed in Detroit just yesterday?"

"Yes. He told Heffernan he was on his way East to look up a literary agent in New York—when he went into the bathroom and found Parne. He stops right there. Nobody's been able to get another word out of him. Now that looks like dinner." Starr eyed a maid in the drawing-room doorway. "Let's go in."

Keith sat at Lily's left, and Mrs. Forrest faced her directly across the table. The others didn't matter. Lily felt the current of these two interests strongly turned on her. She understood Ida Forrest's perfectly but not so well Lorrimer's. She found it too accomplished, in the sense of something having been already settled and which she had not been consulted about. It was (except that he was seated at her side) reminiscent of the sort of feeling she had had when dining out with Nan's father and with Milton Elser. The feeling of being a wife.

It both saddened and annoyed her. Someday if Lorrimer wanted her to, *still* wanted her to—but he wouldn't. He wouldn't even right now if he could see the pictures which were chasing through her deadened head. She thought: I'm the mother of a girl whom I love more than I love life, who has shot a man, no matter why, no matter with what justice or driven by what sense of appalling fear, and my hands have washed out his blood. She was connected in some way with that man and with an addict who takes morphine. Some maelstrom trapped her.

There were two rubbers of bridge, while the Capehart muted through the background tones of a group of Debussy, while brandy sodas were served, and the party broke up at eleven. Lorrimer drove them home, still in the manner of a husband driving his family home, still implying with every comfortable word and gesture that *that* was settled. He stood in the hall for a while, frosty-cheeked, healthy, so implacably sound, prolonged his good night before Sheffield's visionary eyes and the handsome young cop's black shoe-button ones.

"Tomorrow, Lily, shall the three of us lunch at the club?"

"Thank you, Lorrimer."

"All right with you, Nan?"

"I'll be glad to, Mr. Keith."

"I'll call for you. I'll call for you at one."

"We'll be ready."

"Well—good night, Lily."

"Good night, Lorrimer."

"Nan—"

"Good night, Mr. Keith."

He looked at her dotingly.

"Nan, I'd forgotten that you still curtsy. At nineteen. Not much—but there's a trace of curtsy still there."

"I'm an anachronism, Mr. Keith."

"I honestly think you are. One in wolf's clothing, but of the very nicest sort. "Good night."

The heavy front door closed, shutting Lorrimer and all his world out into the snow, closing Lily in tight with Nan. Lily opened her cape and started peeling a glove. She went over to the handsome young cop. He stood up, and she said, "No one has told me your name."

"It's Suffolk, Mrs. Elser. Roy Suffolk."

"I'm worried about your comfort, Mr. Suffolk."

"Oh, I'll make out all right."

"I'd like Sheffield to show you the kitchen and where things are. He'll leave sandwiches, but you'll want your coffee when you want it, and you'll want it hot."

"Thank you very much, Mrs. Elser."

"Then good night—good night."

Lily went upstairs with Nan. They parted on the landing. Nan went to her rooms. Lily went to hers.

The bed looked awfully good. It had never looked better. Turned-down white percale, smooth as glass, the pillows plumped and wanting to be dented, the wool, the folded satin-covered fleece all said: Come along, forget everything. Kill your thinking apparatus and come to bed.

It didn't work.

Lily understood why. Your body and head could get too tired to be tired. Motorcars sometimes used to act that way, just kept on running for a while even after the ignition had been shut off. From residue, searing heat. Which was sometimes also why they exploded or burst into flame after smashing head-on into a blank wall.

Which were no thoughts to put her to sleep.

They all had to be blanked out: Mr. Parne's corpse, the morphine addict, Hangaway, two basins of pinkish water, a thick-lensed chemist testing for human blood, Ida Forrest's bitten, hardened eyes with their defensive frosts and Lorrimer. And Nan's connection with the whole sickening mess.

By one o'clock the thoughts were still alive and eagerly active in the profound hush of the sleeping house. No, Nan wouldn't be sleeping, and neither would that handsome young patrolman Suffolk. Well, maybe he would: it was a fundamental rule of the service that every watchman only remained awake when he was not on guard.

Lily turned on the bed lamp. It was still close enough after one not to matter. You could walk, of course; just up and down the room in slippers and a wrapper until you stumbled and tripped yourself-to sleep. Oke. She liked "Oke." The boy at the filling station used it, and he had a face like a bright red impulsive apple.

She had to see Nan. That was at the base of her not being able to sleep. Right now she had to face her own daughter just as last night she had steeled herself into a determination to face Mr. Parne. Lily stopped short and stared. It seemed that Nan must have had the same thought too.

The hall door of the bedroom was opening. It was the click of the latch which had told her so, strangely sharp and metallic because of the imponderable stillness of the night.

"Nan darling? I'm awake. Come in."

Mr. Hangaway hesitated on the threshold, looking at her.

Mr. Hangaway stepped softly into the room.

He closed the door.

CHAPTER 3

Hangaway was in no hurry. He had all of the time in the world and didn't bother with any further movement after shutting the door but just stood quietly and contemplated Lily with his shiny bright eyes.

Lily didn't make any move either. She couldn't. Within the drained and terrible empty feeling of her body her mind suggested several impossibilities. Each held an ultimate conclusion in Hangaway's death, because that struck her as the only state in which safety lay for any of them: the one sure defense against his glitter.

While he continued to contemplate her Lily's mind considered the job in detail: you shot or stabbed or hit when you wanted to kill somebody, and the first two methods were out. As far as that went so was the last. The fragility of bric-a-brac and *objets d'art* with which Milton had so lovingly bedizened Lily's room would simply strike Mr. Hangaway as funny and serve as stinging goads to thrill him toward his purpose.

That left her hands. It also left the tigress which Starr had sensed in Lily earlier in the day, crouched and desperate for her cub.

Hangaway seemed satisfied with his leisurely observation and finished with it. "I'm glad you're being sensible, Mrs. Elser. Screaming women irritate me. That flatfoot downstairs was good enough to let me in. He won't bother us any."

The vagueness of his statement chilled her, with its definite demolishment of that bridge of escape, the slender hope that young patrolman Suffolk might have been in the kitchen making coffee and might, under the emergency of a scream, come to their help.

She forced herself to look unflinchingly at Hangaway, thinking: This man is a drug addict. Never, for an instant, let his apparent quietness deceive you. And don't corner him. Somewhere, Lily reflected, she had picked up the recipe. Because if you cornered them they never hesitated any longer but just struck. Maybe that only applied to maniacs and referred to humoring them. Maybe you couldn't humor an addict.

"What can I do for you, Mr. Hangaway?"

"Well, I don't know. I mean I can't be specific because I'm not absolutely sure myself."

"Will you excuse me for a moment? I'll change into a house dress—"

"Just hold it, Mrs. Elser. Sit down." He nodded sleepily toward a slipper chair and then nodded again with faint approval as Lily sank into it. "Quit figuring out ways for leaving this room, because that irritates me too."

Hangaway stepped unhurriedly over to the foot of the bed and sat down on it, sticking out his pipe-like ankles and shoving his thin hands deep into overcoat pockets.

"Where's the girl's room, Mrs. Elser?"

"Delilah? She and Sheffield—"

"Don't get smart! The kid."

"My daughter is spending the night with friends."

Hangaway sighed.

"Look, Mrs. Elser. Among other things I've got a gun. See?" He took a service revolver from a pocket and showed it to Lily, then put it back in the pocket. "I took it away from young Handsome downstairs after I knocked him out. I used a tire iron, so I wouldn't go expecting him to be bright for quite a while. What you've got to realize is that I've got something on my mind and I don't want to be"—he searched thoughtfully for the precise word—"to be brooked."

"No—of course not, Mr. Hangaway."

"And don't humor me. I know what you're feeling and what you're thinking, and you're wrong. You're wrong about what you're thinking, at least. The kid doesn't mean a thing to me that way. Not so much as *that*!"

He snapped skeleton fingers and glittered at her earnestly. Curiously Lily believed him, and a tide of relief flooded through her until she remembered that remark of Starr's before dinner concerning addicts: It's one of their main dangers. They lull you with their pleasantries into a false security before, well, the other side of them comes out.

Not that Hangaway's attitude of abnegation toward Nan was a pleasantry, but it had undoubtedly been offered to put her at ease. This was a thought which forced Lily to stifle a hysterical laugh.

"I amuse you, Mrs. Elser?"

"I assure you that you don't."

"You're lying, but it's quite all right. You know how repulsive I'd be to your daughter or to you for that matter. No women care for me much, not with any real feeling. It's because of the way I look. I've gotten quite used to it."

The voice *was* lulling and held none of the strong strident tones of Hangaway's morning performances. Rather it flowed reasonably, with reason, and Lily found herself saying with a desperate calmness, "I think you are being unfair to yourself Mr. Hangaway."

"No. I know. Whenever I want any love I've got to take it. It's never given to me. Nothing's ever been given to me, Mrs. Elser. I suppose you'll think this funny but as a kid I had to steal the milk my mother thought I ought to drink. She was a terrible slut. I can't remember her ever having been sober, except on the night, when she killed the man she said was my father. He was quite a package himself. Was a college professor once. I never did know exactly what they canned him for, but you only needed a couple of guesses after you'd looked at him. They made a great team all right. You mustn't think I'm asking for sympathy."

"No, certainly not."

"I'm too old for it. I was too old for it at birth. The point is just this, Mrs. Elser. I always had to take things. Everything. Now it's a habit. Which room is the kid's?"

"My daughter is spending the night with the Tomlinsons, Mr. Hangaway."

He sighed again.

"I *did* tell you that I don't want to be brooked."

The repetition of the phrase pleased him, but in the light of a practical example of his distaste at obstructions it struck him as rather weak. It left a lack of a proper appreciation of his power. His strong and serviceable power. He got up from the foot of the bed and stepped softly over to the slipper chair and then, still softly, kissed Lily on the lips.

"You don't like that do you, Mrs. Elser?" He bit her cheek sharply and, with a skeleton hand, almost succeeded in stifling her cry. "Now that sort of treatment you don't mind so much. Just take it easy. Write it off as a lesson in behavior. You see I understand women like you pretty well. You can take a beating easier than you can take a kiss on the mouth."

Hangaway idly observed the tiny blood bead on Lily's cheek, her tight trembling.

"I know the gun didn't impress you," he said, "but I think that that object lesson will. It's funny how little you realize what worlds we are apart. You in orderly fields and me in a jungle. Oh, I've no illusion about myself, none whatever. Your sort of life, love on rose leaves, I'd simply get no kick out of it. I *like* it to be sordid, illicit, in caves of darkness, obscure corners of a barn. Wipe your cheek off. There's blood on it. Go ahead. I'll let you."

Lily stood up and went to a dresser. She took a handkerchief from a drawer and pressed it to her cheek. There was a nail file with a silver handle among the articles on the dresser. Lily covered it with the blood-spotted handkerchief, looking at Hangaway's very bright eyes as they stared in reflection at her in the mirror. "I doubt if you'd know where to put it," he said.

"I beg your pardon?"

"The nail file, Mrs. Elser. People have such funny notions about vital spots. They seem to think that all you have to do is to stick something sharp into a man's body and he dies. Now I've seen a man with fifteen or sixteen stab wounds in him before anything happened of any importance. They used ice picks, and even then he almost got well. That wasn't because he was tough but simply because the job was sloppy. Wait—"

He held up bony fingers and shook one warningly, while both of them listened to the rapping on the door, then to Nan's voice saying: "Mother, are you all right? Did you call just now?"

Lily did not stop to think, to figure anything out, There wasn't anything you could figure, beyond trying to block Mr. Hangaway. Surely just the sheer weight of your body would act as an anchor, and you could stick for at least as long as you could breathe. She threw herself at him and clung to him in her great despair, without much to cling to but his overcoat, which bunched softly in her hands and felt slippery.

"Nan darling—run—*run—get out of the house*—get help—"

Hangaway looked down at Lily derisively and disentangled her arms like threads; then he cupped his fingers tight over her mouth and pressed cruelly and shoved her hard backward, and sent her staggering backward into the slipper chair. He opened the hall door.

"Come on in, Miss Elser."

Nan stood and looked at him, while her face changed from bewilderment into horror, into the terror of comprehension. She ran past him, straight to Lily, and cowered down on her knees by the chair, while that animal look of fright was in her eyes, the helpless look of stark dread, and her voice shook.

"What's he doing here? What's he doing to you, Mother?"

"Nothing—just be quiet, darling."

Nan said to Hangaway, so weakly that it seemed silly to expect him to hear her, "What are you doing here?"

He shut the hall door and sat down on the foot of the bed again, idly observing the two tense, shaking women, pleased with the picture in its satisfactory presentation of utter rout before his remarkable power. The kid's voice was as it should be, too: a proper bleat. A very pretty dish. Maybe, if there was time, he'd see how he felt about it.

"Well, as I said to your mother, I don't exactly know. I tell you what, Miss Elser. We'll start with Detroit. Just what gave you the first lead?"

"I don't know what you're talking about."

He looked pained. She was obviously going to be irritating. Maybe she would need an object lesson like the one he'd given her mother. Her check was very fresh and very inviting. So was her neck. Sock the old one cold first naturally.

"I've gone to some trouble to explain to your mother that I don't like being irritated, Miss Elser. I'm after information and I won't be brooked. How did you get wise to Worthby Haines?"

"I don't know him."

"Well, this looks like it's going to be tough. How much did you shake him down for?"

Lily said fiercely, seeing what she saw in Hangaway's eyes and no longer caring how foul the maelstrom might have been, "Tell him anything. Tell him anything, darling, that he wants to know. You know that I love you, darling. Will always love you, darling."

"But I've nothing to tell, Mother."

"Why don't you listen to her, Miss Elser? She's giving you good advice. You can't handle this thing right, not alone. Even if your mother's in on it with you, you'll both end up short, Haines is hard—as you know. He'd see to it that somebody wrapped you up in cement just as quick as he'd pick a daisy. You'd better turn the proof over to me."

He stood up suddenly and you hardly noticed him moving, but he was beside them, leaning down with his big bony head, and he reached out and touched Nan's cheek with a finger.

He said with a stealthy softness. "Did Parne get them last night and hide them?"

His finger went on stroking Nan's check experimentally, like a fleshless bone making circles on a peach. It felt downy and soft to him, and he thought: Power *is* everything in life.

Power was way beyond bodily perfection and pretty looks in the things it could get you. He was glad that he wasn't pretty. Pretty boys never got anything much for themselves because too many people wanted them and they didn't last. Decay set in quick, and then they were sunk and everybody who had liked them gave them the go-by and looked around for something fresher. Sometimes it even discouraged them into suicide, and they killed themselves as a last grab after the limelight and being important.

He said again, "*Did* Parne get them, Miss Elser?"

"I don't know."

"You don't know Worthby Haines?"

"No."

"You didn't know Parne?"

"No."

He said with quiet indifference, "You're a liar, Miss Elser."

"Oh, tell him, darling—*tell him.*"

"She will."

"I can't."

Nan's shaking increased, and sobs suddenly choked her. Lily thought: She is lying about Mr. Parne. That much I know. Maybe I'm the one who's keeping her from talking. Just by being here.

Hangaway seemed suddenly to lose interest in them. He was thinking: Now what does that black ape want?

"I've telephoned for the police, ma'am."

"Sheffield—go—go—"

He stood uncertainly in the hall doorway, with a great sense of dignity all touching him, with his vague eyes staring from their distant past into a far more distant future, out of that black and old, serene face.

"So you have phoned for the police."

"Yes sir, Mr. Hangaway."

Hangaway went to a window and looked out upon the dark, snow-laced sky, on the white silence of the ground, into the whole deathlike hush of the shrouded night. There was no hurry. Even if the police had been able to make it with dog teams they could no more put a finger on him than they could on an elemental force. Still it was irritating. These bothersome little people all harassing him.

"You—Sheffield—come over here."

"Yes sir."

"No, come right over. Come real close."

"Yes sir."

"I guess you're pretty pleased with yourself."

"I wouldn't know, sir."

"I don't mean about the police."

"No sir."

"I mean about coining in here like this." Hangaway's voice slipped into a sneering purr. "To offer your protection to the ladies."

Hangaway thoughtfully considered Sheffield's old face for quite a while. It seemed all lighted up, strangely, through its blackness. A dumb and patient glow. Hangaway sank his fist with plenty of satisfaction into the face.

He left the room.

* * * *

The chair was a recipe too: tilted at an angle and its top wedged under the knob of the door. A Chippendale guardian between them and Mr. Hangaway until after a battle through the snows, the police would arrive.

Lily pressed a cold cloth on Sheffield's face, which was a dark oval on her lap, and thought: That's a foolish notion and I guess I must be crazy. I wanted him out of here more than anything on earth. But I've got to be honest. I felt that way about him, in terror about him, only up to the moment when I didn't know what he had come here for. When I thought he was simply driven by a drug-crazed lust for attack and violence. Then he started in on Detroit. That was the time when it really got bad. You could always push a thing a little way back into your mind as long as you really didn't know. While actual words still hadn't been spoken like a plain No or Yes.

Or before you had been faced with a positive lie.

"Darling—a cold one, please."

Nan took the towel.

"Yes, Mother."

The lie was such an inescapable light. Nan *had* known Parne. It shone its bitter illuminating gleam on all the rest. Nan had shot Parne, because certainly Mr. Hangaway had not. You could pin a good deal on addicts, but there was a limit.

There could be no sane or insane reason for Hangaway to have come to the house in the morning, to have returned for his obscure purpose tonight (with its inclusive assault on the law) if *he* had killed Parne. Because he would have gotten what he wanted at the time of the murder. What he wanted and what Parne had wanted.

What Nan still had?

"Thank you, darling."

"Mother."

"Darling?"

"Oh, why don't they hurry? Why don't they get here?"

"They will, dear. The roads. The drifts, I imagine."

The photograph loomed impressively in Lily's sickened thoughts: the Endermann & Endermann's Detroit branch cabinet portrait of Nan, with her hair on the top of her head, with a younger look of the summer-in-Cleveland period of two years ago. It was important, the picture. It had to be. Otherwise Mr. Parne wouldn't have carried it, buried it beneath the things in his Gladstone. And otherwise (what else could you think?) Mr. Parne might not have been killed. Sheffield made faint sounds and opened his eyes.

"I'se sorry, ma'am."

"I'll never be able to repay you, Sheffield."

"Thank you, ma'am."

He made great efforts and stood up, swaying a little and resting palsied fingers on a chair.

"Does it hurt much, Sheffield?"

"No ma'am. It don't hurt me now, not at all."

Lily's fingers clenched.

"I could kill that man with pleasure."

She caught Nan's swift, odd glance, and then Nan went back into the bathroom with the cold wet towel.

Sheffield wandered toward the hall door.

"With your permission, ma'am? I is worried about Delilah."

"How cruel—how thoughtless of me. We'll all go, Sheffield."

"I'se done left her when I grew uneasy and suspected that I heared the sounds."

"Nan, darling, we'll stay close together, the three of us."

"No ma'am. You jest put the chair back under the knob when I is gone."

Lily reflected that it was extraordinary, honestly, what profound fright gripped her at the thought of being alone with Nan. Unreasonable, unnatural and sheer, but there it was.

"I feel certain that Mr. Hangaway will have left the house, Sheffield."

"I does feel that way also, ma'am."

"Come, Nan." Lily removed the chair. "We'll go."

She led them along the lighted hall. It was inimical in spite of its lights, peopled in its air and deep hush with brooding, angry wraiths whipped from dark fastnesses of the brain. Lily walked swiftly, feeling Nan and Sheffield close behind her, up the stairs, and opened a door into a room where a bed lamp cast long shadows.

"Delilah—are you all right?"

Delilah looked queer, sitting up on the bed, clutching a bright pink nightgown tight about her withered body.

"I feel a touch of the misery, madam."

"Did Mr. Hangaway come in here?"

Delilah's eyes, in spite of their sharp intent, managed to look vague.

"I did not know the gentleman was here, madam."

Lily felt an obscure uneasiness about the immediate moment. She studied Delilah's blank, reserved face and could read nothing, any more than she'd ever been able to. She said, "We feel reasonably certain that he has left the house. The police will be here shortly." (You simply *didn't* use such phrases.) "Is there something wrong, Delilah? Are you certain that you feel all right?"

"Yes, madam. ' Her eyes were veiled again, staring a long way off at nothing. "If madam will excuse me for not getting up?"

"Of course, Delilah. I'm telephoning Doctor Starr. I believe it's quite safe to leave you." (Was it? *Was* it?) "We must see what we can do for the patrolman. We don't know how badly he may have been hurt."

"Yes, madam."

The nagging doubt increased.

"Just the same—I think after we leave I'd bolt the door."

"I will, madam."

The queer procession recurred through the night-filled, silent house, with Lily silently leading, leading two mutes. The front door stood ajar, letting in soft vagrant flakes of snow on the chill night air. Young Suffolk lay sprawled on his face on the floor. A tire tool was beside him. There was some blood. His breathing was heavy and painful. You could hear it with extraordinary clarity through the hush.

Lily said with intuitive correctness, "I think it's serious and we'd better not move him. Close the door, Sheffield. Cover him with blankets. Keep him warm." Lily went to a telephone in the cloakroom. She dialed Starr's number, and he answered directly.

"This is Lily Elser, Doctor."

His voice was immediately awake, greatly concerned.

"Yes, Mrs. Elser."

"Mr. Suffolk, the policeman on guard here, has been struck on the head by Mr. Hangaway. I don't like his breathing."

"Are you safe? Is Miss Elser safe?"

"Yes. He's gone. We found the front door ajar. The police are on the way."

"I'll start at once. I'll arrange for an ambulance and have them get things ready at the hospital. It sounds like concussion."

"Thank you, Doctor. Is there anything we can do right now?"

"Nothing. Don't move him. Keep him warm."

"Yes, Doctor."

There was a small couch in the cloakroom, a brief affair, smugly elegant in striped satin. Lily lay down on it. She lost consciousness as her head touched it.

* * * *

Dr. Starr and Mr. Heffernan were both there.

Dr. Starr was sitting beside the bed. Mr. Heffernan was standing at one of the windows with his back to it, looking across a shadowed space of room straight at her. Lily saw small sympathy in his look and for a moment thought it odd.

"How is Nan, Doctor?"

"Fine, Mrs. Elser. I'd say she was tough as a brick if it made any sense, but it doesn't. How about you?"

"I'm afraid I fainted."

"You did. You've been up here for a couple of hours."

"Delilah? Sheffield? That poor young policeman?"

"The misery, a bad bruise and a slight concussion. It was an outrage to get me out of bed."

Lily smiled back, feeling restless through her weakness and at a disadvantage lying down like this. She sat up and went into immediate attack against the look in Heffernan's steady eyes.

"Have you caught him, Mr. Heffernan?"

He stayed by the window, just straightening a little into a stance of more rigorous formality, with stiff shoulders and with stiffness in his voice: entirely a different man.

"Not yet, Mrs. Elser. We know he must still be in the vicinity. Nothing is moving. The roads going out of town are completely blocked."

Starr touched Lily's pulse, smiled at her reassuringly.

"Is it wise to talk? Are you sure it wouldn't be better just to rest?"

"But I feel splendid, Doctor."

"Very well. Mr. Heffernan is somewhat anxious. He has an impression that you can tell him a few things. Don't let him tire you out. Quote me if you feel he is doing so. Just look at him frigidly and say, 'Doctor's orders.'"

"Thank you, Doctor."

"I will join you in my living room in a moment, Mr. Heffernan."

"Thank you, Mrs. Elser."

He bowed slightly, stiffly, and went into the adjoining room, closing the bedroom door. Lily took off the wrapper and slipped into a tea gown, got into stockings, slippers, made swift slight repairs to her hair. The mirror showed her the marks which had been left on her cheek by Hangaway's teeth. She saw that Dr. Starr must have disinfected them, and he had given them a coating of newskin.

I'm afraid I fainted. You did. You've been up here for a couple of hours.

Just what, during those two hours, had Nan said? How much had she told? How solidly by now was District Attorney Heffernan entrenched in Detroit? Lily's own special problem never occurred to her, except in its possible repercussions on Nan. Had the child held to her grimly desperate refusal to speak? It was the premise upon which Lily felt it safer to act.

She went into the living room and found him still standing, stiffly formal. There was no shred of concern in his manner for her, for the appalling experience which she had just been through. He was a portrait of himself, brushed woodenly on canvas by a third-rate hack.

"Will you smoke, Mr. Heffernan?"

She held out a cloisonné box.

"Thank you, Mrs. Elser."

He lighted her cigarette and waited for her to sit down, then permitted himself to be fitted.

"I'm curious to know how Mr. Hangaway escaped from the hospital, Mr. Heffernan."

"It simply never occurred to them that he would. Or that he wanted to." Heffernan took two polite puffs and then crushed out the cigarette. "Nor did it occur to anybody that he would come back here."

"I rather wish that it had."

At long last and reluctantly it dragged out of him.

"We're sorry about that, Mrs. Elser."

"Have you ever read about typhoon? Either that book of Conrad's or that one by Hughes about Jamaica?"

"I've read Conrad's, yes, Mrs. Elser."

"The strongest impression they gave me was that a relatively brief stretch of time could seem so never-ending. Both books dealt with a question of hours, and yet the feeling was one of an eternity while the storm approached to its height, there was the central lull and the storm went away."

"You mean that Mr. Parne was killed only yesterday morning, and still?"

"I mean exactly that. The part that terrified me most in both of those books, Mr. Heffernan, was the lull."

"Yes, there is something frightening in feeling that you've got to face the same thing through again."

"Quite frightening."

"Just why do you feel that way now, Mrs. Elser?"

"Perhaps because I've had no sleep."

"Only that?"

Lily said with helpless sharpness, "Just how far do you think that nerves can stretch, Mr. Heffernan?"

"I'm terribly sorry." At the moment he meant it. But the moment was brief, and he was all stiff again. "I'm sorry about this, having to ask you things when I know that you need rest. It's my job. I'm one of the people who are being paid to find out why Parne was killed and by whom."

"Naturally, and as a matter of fact I don't feel awfully tired. I suppose after you've had no sleep for more than—"

Red flowed slowly up across her checks, and Heffernan said patiently, "For more than how many hours, Mrs. Elser?"

"It's again the typhoon. Actually I've only been up since eight yesterday morning, but there you are—I feel aged enough to be a stand-in for Methuselah."

He refused to be amused.

"You have already told me that you heard no sound during the night before last. Was that because you slept without waking?"

"Yes. Mr. Parne said good night to my daughter and to me about eleven, and Delilah woke me at eight."

"I would like to go back to Mr. Parne's arrival here in the house."

"Yes?"

"You see, Mrs. Elser, we have had to give up the thought that Hangaway had anything to do with Parne's death."

"You could find no connections between them?"

"No, it isn't that. That angle may still be there. It's an alibi. I believe you know that filling station about a mile or so north of here."

"Yes—Oke's."

"Oke?"

"That's what I call the boy who runs it."

"Well, he read about Hangaway in the evening papers. They carried a good description of Hangaway, also one of those press snapshots. The boy came and saw me around ten o'clock, after he got off. He said Hangaway had stopped over at the filling station from four in the morning until about half-past seven, when he left for here. Hangaway drank a lot of black coffee and went to sleep in the station."

"Simply no tradition is safe nowadays."

"I know it. He asked the boy quite a lot of questions, Mrs. Elser. He asked him how to get to this house."

"But why?"

"I don't know. When he found out that the boy sometimes serviced your car Hangaway also asked him if your daughter was home, Mrs. Elser."

"That is odder—it is more absurd still."

"Yes, it would seem so, but he did. The boy said he didn't seem to act as if he knew your daughter but just was interested as to whether she was home or not. The boy told Hangaway he hadn't seen her and that as far as he knew she was still in Detroit."

"I am positive that Nan knows nothing about him."

"Yes, Miss Elser has told us that she doesn't. Either about Hangaway or Parne. It's quite puzzling. I understand that Parne got here about four o'clock in the afternoon."

"Yes."

He said suddenly, miserably, with the years and all his stiffness dropping away and leaving him naked in his teens, "Can't you see how I hate all this? Questioning you, shaking out all the whole damned bag of tricks in my job? I've always admired you, Mrs. Elser, and I guess that's stronger than merely liking a person. There's something very right and fine about you, and I can say the same thing about your daughter. Will you be honest with me? Will you make things easier for me by being so?"

She felt better, happier and then infinitely worse. Lily wanted to tell him everything, not only every act but every feeling and thought and fear that she had endured during the past wretched hours. She wanted to do so not so much because it would make her feel better but because she thought it would make him feel better. To repay him for this abrupt letting down of the bars and this friendly show on his part of wanting to do her a kindness.

Reason checked the flood of; words welling up in Lily, and she thought: I'm a selfish fool. I can't say a thing without endangering the child I love. Just a couple of words of truth and I might as well never have given her birth, never have fought and struggled through those early tormenting years, never have shaped my course with her as the star to set it by.

She said coldly, "If you will tell me a little more clearly just what you want to know, Mr. Heffernan. I am sure you will understand my being somewhat confused."

It was a blow in the face in a way, and he felt it like that, a dash of icy water which made him grow implacable, whereas before he had just felt officially hard.

"I want to know the moves you made concerning Parne's room after he got here, Mrs. Elser."

"Moves? But I still don't understand. Delilah arranged the rooms, and Sheffield showed Mr. Parne to his."

"Then we are to understand that you yourself were never in Parne's room?" Lily thought swiftly: He's all business now. I've both antagonized and hurt him. I left fingerprints in the room beyond the ones on the doorknobs—perhaps on Mr. Parne's luggage when I found Nan's picture. I wiped the gun, the doorknobs, but not the luggage.

"No, I naturally went up to see whether everything was in order, Mr. Heffernan.

"Was this after Parne came?"

"Yes. It was after Sheffield had taken Mr. Parne's bags upstairs. While they were both putting the ear into the garage. I thought it better to check on towels, linen, the usual things. It's so long since we have used the rooms in the north wing." Lily smiled brightly. "I believe I even became a porter for an instant and moved Mr. Parne's bags from the floor to the luggage stand."

"Yes."

(So it had been the bags. He knew that: that she had touched them.)

He said after a moment, "That would have been shortly after four o'clock in the afternoon. Did you return to the room later on, Mrs. Elser?"

"Later? Why?"

"I should like to know."

"There was no occasion to, Mr. Heffernan."

"Then you want us to understand that the next time you were there was after Hangaway had told you about finding Parne dead?"

"Yes."

"Would you mind details?"

"No, of course not."

"Tell me what you did that time."

"Why I just looked in, then I telephoned to Doctor Starr and the police."

"No—please—more in detail, please."

"But how?"

"I want to know where you stood, how far into the room you walked, how close you went to Parne. That's what I want, Mrs. Elser."

Lily was deeply puzzled and clammy with fright. That was all she *had* done: just stood in the doorway and looked at Parne, briefly renewing her impression of the picture which she knew so well. But it was obvious that Mr. Heffernan felt that some further move had occurred, something on which he seemed to be placing a wealth of importance. Well, at least with this instance she could stick rigidly to the truth.

"I did not go into the room at all, Mr. Heffernan. I stood in the doorway, as I say, and went no further."

He looked at her with a curious mixture of contempt and pity. There was a dash of horror, too, of the fascinated sort, when suddenly in a lovely garden you observe the placid sunning of a pretty snake. He stood up and for an instant seemed embarrassed.

"Well, thank you, Mrs. Elser. And good night."

"Good night, Mr. Heffernan."

* * * *

Ida Forrest heard the faint sound of the telephone bell and was instantly awake. There was only one instrument in the house, downstairs in what had been her husband's (Jason's) study and which was now Gene's, except that Gene never used it. This always faintly irked Ida because she had an orderly mind and liked activities, as well as things, to be in their proper niches.

The telephone went on ringing.

Ida hoped that Gene would not hear it. Normally he would not, as he slept like a log, but Dr. Starr's dinner party had been upsetting emotionally, because of its dark undercurrents, and Gene might easily be spending a restless sleepless night.

It continued to ring.

Ida knew it would be connected in some fashion with the Elsers. The hour was after three, which automatically divorced the call from ordinary social or business matters and shoved it into the perquisites of drama.

The bell stopped on the seventh ring.

Either they had hung up or Gene was downstairs answering it, because the regular number of rings was ten. Ida sat upright, in the strictest of nightgowns, and listened more intently. Her hearing was remarkably acute, and soon she caught a faint and remote rumble of Gene's voice. She got out of bed and put on crocheted slippers and a woolen bathrobe and went out into the cold hall.

Ida's eyes were sharp and frosty with concern, and she said as he came hurrying up the stairs, "What was it, Gene?"

"Lorrimer Keith, Mother."

"At this hour?" (It was strange, but then it wasn't really. Besides being an executor of her estate, Lorrimer's sheep's eyes at Lily during dinner had been obvious enough: the connection with high drama still held.) "What does he want?"

"He's at the Elsers'."

Ida stepped back to let him join her on the landing and said impatiently, "Of course he is, but what does he want with you?"

"He thinks I ought to be there."

"Why?"

"Mr. Keith said he was worried about the situation."

"What situation? Why is he there at this hour anyway?"

"The dope fiend got loose and broke in."

"Mercy!"

"Yes."

"*Mercy!*"

"He only knocked the cop out. It isn't that."

"What isn't?"

"It's business, Mother."

"Well, what business?"

"Mr. Keith thinks I ought to be on hand in case they need advice."

"I do wish you'd make sense, Gene. You're not Lorrimer's lawyer, and you certainly aren't the Elsers'."

"I know it. That's just why."

"Why haven't you got your bathrobe on? And no slippers. Why is it just why?"

"Because Mr. Keith thinks I could be there as a friend, just pretend that I came because I was worried about what happened to them and still be handy to give them legal advice. He doesn't want to bring old Wellburn into it because it would be too obvious—show that they were scared."

"What *did* happen, Gene?"

"Nothing, as I told you, Mother, but Mr. Keith is a little uneasy about the district attorney's attitude."

"Mercy! Then there was—then she did—"

"No there wasn't and she didn't. It's just an attitude. I've got to dress, Mother."

"Gene, I don't want you to go'"

"No, I figured you wouldn't. But I'm going, Mother."

"Then I'm going with you."

"No."

Ida permitted the line to run out a little.

"But it will be perfectly all right, Gene. I shall simply be doing what I can for Lily Elser. Her friends must stand by her at a time like this."

"Mrs. Elser is asleep."

"I'll be ready by the time you get the car around, dear."

"I'm not taking you, Mother. This is business."

* * * *

Starr watched Keith set the scene. He liked Keith and enjoyed him: liked his substantial, fine qualities and was amused by his foibles. He considered Keith's habit of dramatizing his several selves as a good thing, as an excellent safety valve against repressions: the banker president, the suave clubman, the modest (but still par) golfer and—right now—the old boy, standing by.

Standing by Lily Elser.

He thanked Keith for replenishing his brandy and soda and watched Keith replenish his own and then return his buttocks for further toasting before the logs. The stage at last seemed right: intimate, slightly conspiratorial, very man to man.

Starr wondered just how far by Lily Elser Keith would stand. He would see her through, of course. There was no doubt about that. But what then? What about after the bitter sequences which seemed inevitable? The arrest, the arraignment, the grand jury with its indictment, the waiting weeks in jail, the trial?

Then the verdict.

Starr held no illusions about Heffernan's opinion or Heffernan's purpose: all of the sordid sequences were intended to occur. The case against Lily Elser was closed with the exception of some single link. Undoubtedly there lay in Heffernan's possession the most damning of evidence and clues, painstakingly documented and weighed and ready to strike her down with like a club on the moment when that last link should be obtained.

It was a bond, Starr believed, which would tie her understandably to Parne, one without which the state's case was likely to collapse, because in that bond must be the motive for the crime.

Keith started his obliques.

"How frequently, Colin, you can paraphrase Hamlet."

"To talk or not to talk? That is her problem?"

"Yes, and I'm afraid we must consider that it truly is. I honestly don't know what to advise Lily to do. I'm sure we both agree that Heffernan is a very sound, a very intelligent man."

"Also an open-minded and a just one."

"Yes, and it's quite obvious that he is simply waiting, just marking time."

"For the link? You feel that too?"

"For whatever it is that connects Lily with those men. We've got to face that, of course—the fact that neither Parne nor Hangaway came to this house through any chance."

"Why specifically Mrs. Elser, Lorrimer? Have you thought of the possibility that the tie-up might lie through her daughter?"

"Nan? Absurd. She's a child."

"No, not any longer. Up to the time when she left for Detroit, if you wish. She's a woman now."

"Oh, come, she's only nineteen."

"That was Mrs. Elser's age when Nan was born."

"Well, you're right. It had never occurred to me."

Keith reviewed his private images and did not want them changed: Lily *had* to remain a gracious, lovable woman with whom, side by side, he would spend his remaining years, and Nan had to remain a charming daughter already fully grown.

Desperately, above all else, Keith wanted no link to exist between either of them and Parne, even if the crime were to remain forever vague. At any costs he wanted no dirty brush to smear its grime on Lily. He wanted the past from where such a brush would naturally arise to stay battened down and dead.

He said to Starr, "We may need your help. I don't mean medically; I mean in the way you've handled those other criminal cases around town."

"Gladly, Lorrimer."

"Thank you, Colin. Although I don't know what under the sun you could do."

"I don't myself. The medico-legal angles of Parne's death were childishly obvious." Starr added uncomfortably, "They lacked the most elementary professional touch."

"I know what you mean. But we'll fight up to the last. And even then."

"Of course."

"Does nothing strike you? Nothing at all?"

Starr said again, "Only Nan."

"No, I can't. I won't believe it."

"And I cannot eliminate the thought. It persists in nagging me. Look here, you play chess, don't you?"

"Yes."

"Well, then think of your pawns."

It was then that they heard the scream.

* * * *

He, too, as Parne had been, was freshly dead.

He was a well-built man in his late forties, conservatively, expensively dressed, with a stubble of beard on his chin and a dusty, rumpled look about his clothing. He lay on his back just as Parne had lain, and his eyelids were slightly opened, showing crescents of an oyster white. A black hole in his temple oozed blood. He was not lying, as Parne had been, across the bathroom sill but was stretched at length between the bed and one of the windows.

Blankets and sheets lay in a heap on the floor. The mattress had been slit in a dozen places from which its stuffings had been explored and pulled. The pillows were half empty of their feathers.

There were two guns. One was gripped in the dead man's hand. The other was in Nan's.

Only the bed lamp burned.

Lily reached the room first, the room which for a single night had been Mr. Parne's. She had caught the sound of footsteps pounding up the broad curved stairs as she had run past the landing. She would have one instant of grace out of eternity, while they determined where to look for the source of the scream.

Lily took the gun out of Nan's hand and held it in her own. It's metal felt warm to the touch, and cordite still was a slight and acrid tang in the air. She opened a window swiftly and threw the gun far out into the banks of snow, then closed the window and gathered Nan tightly into her arms. She murmured incoherently, "Be still, darling. Say nothing. Be still, my dear—be still—"

Gene's shout brought the other two men, brought Sheffield but not (the thought struck Lily briefly) Delilah. It was a stilted scene which revolved around and before Lily slowly in a stunned sort of confusion. Starr on a knee by the body, examining, pronouncing the man dead. Gene and Lorrimer looking blankly stricken. And only Sheffield looking dispassionate and tired.

Starr stood up and said gravely, "Do you know who this is, Mrs. Elser?"

Lily hadn't looked. She went closer to the body, and Nan still clung to her, moving the few steps as she moved, clinging to her in a torment of intermittent shaking. Lily looked. It was funny to be able to stand there quietly and look not at the man so much as through him and, through that filter, backward and further backward through the years. Heavier solider, more flesh about the jowls but, yes, she knew him.

"He is Nan's father, Doctor."

So, Starr thought, the link.

CHAPTER 4

Well, then, here was the end.

All of the swing through the past nineteen years was over, and there Lily felt herself right back at the start. With Robert. Plumper, jowlier, less excitingly feral and dead, but still Robert. She reflected on its cruelty and deep injustice: that a biological trap which so many years ago had sprung and inflicted its scars should have the power once more to reopen them.

Lily thanked Starr for the tablet, for the glass of water, and leaned back with a lassitude of dead indifference on the chaise-lounge in her upstairs living room, her face pallid and oddly serene against a champagne-toned French corduroy. Starr drew a chair up close. He offered Lily a cigarette for which she thanked him and refused.

"Our time may be brief, Mrs. Elser."

"I know that, Doctor."

"I have told Lorrimer that I will do everything I can."

Lily was vaguely glad that he should want to and that Lorrimer should have asked him. It was terribly difficult to try and concentrate.

"Doctor Starr, do you believe in fate?"

"Yes."

"You do? You, a physician, believe in it?"

"Fate is a term," he said, "that scientists hold in a bondage of disrepute, simply for the protection of their precious formulas and equations. They insist on the inflexible rule. It's their mental as well as their physical bread and butter."

"Physicians also?"

"Yes, to a lesser degree. I'm sometimes inclined to wonder whether the alchemists and the Magians didn't pull off a sounder job than we do, by kissing the occult on both cheeks whereas we only peck at one of them—but for heaven's sake, don't quote me."

Lily smiled faintly.

"I shan't. Well, I am a victim of it."

"I felt so obscurely. As I say, we've little time. There are many confusions." Starr added earnestly, "Won't you clear them for me, Mrs. Elser?"

"I think you ought to know that I did not tell a literal lie when I came here. There was a basis of probability of reason."

"When you came to Laurel Falls?"

"Yes, sixteen years ago. I called myself a widow. I had begun to hope, in fact, to feel an assurance by that time that I was one."

Starr thought: She's getting at it. I still can't press her or she'll dry up. We've only ten or fifteen minutes at the best.

"You believed that your husband, that Robert Warden was dead?"

"It was kinder to. Much kinder."

"Why, Mrs. Elser?"

"He left me on the night that Nan was born. He said, 'You're certainly sweating, Lily,' and he said to the woman who was helping out, 'Isn't she? Enough to float a ship.' And he went out, slamming the door. He always slammed the door."

"Yes, Mrs. Elser."

"This will seem funny to you, Doctor, but I never realized until then how much I must have loved him. I knew it because his going hurt, even more than the other."

"And he?"

"Oh, Robert never loved me at all. That's obvious, isn't it?"

"I don't know. There are so many aspects. Any number of things can dam up love temporarily, and still it will flow again if it gets a chance. I've known of cases at childbirth where a man has hated his wife because he was hating himself for what she was going through. Sort of a defense-complex thing. Did you never hear from him?"

"Nothing."

He left her sinking for a moment in this torment of the past and reflected how pointedly Robert Warden's death would motivate Heffernan's case: bigamy—the scandal of it reflected no matter how innocently on Lily and on Nan—no district attorney could want a better handle.

"Did you accept his death as a fact, Mrs. Elser, or did you take any steps to try and prove it?"

"I had a little money, Doctor. Too little for any exhaustive and expensive search. I think that even if I had had a great deal of money I would have been ashamed to use it in that way. I waited for five years and then got a divorce on the grounds of desertion. Naturally the case was uncontested. I waited two more years. Doctor, and then arranged that he be declared legally dead. That was in nineteen twenty-nine, four years before my marriage with Milton."

Starr felt profound relief.

"But, Mrs. Elser, that's splendid. Don't you see? There goes the mainstay of Heffernan's case."

Lily thought: Oh no, it doesn't. It isn't as simple as that. It's as complicated as Parne, as Hangaway, as Detroit, as Robert's dead body, as the three of them all converging out of Detroit and into this house.

As Nan.

"I wish, Doctor, that it could be so."

She was right, of course, and Starr felt his exhilaration draining away, because motives for any murder could be legion whereas authenticated proofs were rare as truth, and Heffernan must hold a lot of them in his hand. He studied Lily's limp indifference toward the deadly urgency of her position.

He thought: We've all been focused on her. She has held us like a strong beam shining in twilight. She has obscured the *mise en scène*.

He thought: Can that be it? *Can that be it?*

* * * *

Heffernan had read several biographies of public executioners and had considered them distasteful to a point that touched on the horrendous. During his two terms in office he had only once (metaphorically) wielded the ax himself. He has asked a jury to give a man a verdict of death. The jury had, and the man was dead. The man had shouted at him: "It's you, not them, that kill me. Just because you are bright."

It was very, very true.

The man had sliced his mistress's throat and slit her stomach and thoroughly deserved an official execution, but Heffernan had not known the well-carved mistress whereas, during the months of waiting and during the weeks of the trial, he had come to know the man. That was what had made the difference by being bright, he had had to kill him.

And now he had to be bright again.

He wondered if when the time came Lily would shout something at him too. The probability seemed incredible, just as did the fact that Lily's loveliness and gentle nature and all-around kindness was nothing but a deceit: a spell woven by the blackest of arts for the confusion and death by violence of (two) men. He felt a little sick when he recalled his surge of fierce joy and high determination upon taking the oath of his office, his bemused and stuffy vision of himself in shining armor, blind, as Justice is blind, to everything but the right.

You couldn't *be* blind about Lily.

She had left the chaise-lounge and was seated in an arm-chair when he had come in. She seemed to be hung on hooks against the back of the chair, a marvelous replica of herself in wax, and stuffed with sawdust. This general effigy effect was further emphasized by her air of disinterestedness both in him and in his secretary, Chester Minkle—a thin young man with lush eyes sitting over at a desk with a thoroughly false attitude of blasé boredom.

Heffernan made his voice purposefully sharp.

"Mrs. Elser."

"Yes?"

"We have reached a point where I am restricted to every legal nicety of my office."

"Yes?"

"I want you to know your rights. I want you to reconsider, if you wish, your decision against having Gene Forrest here to advise you."

"But I still see no reason why I should, Mr. Heffernan."

This irritated him into a gesture of genuine impatience.

"Really, Mrs. Elser. I know why Forrest's here. I know why Lorrimer Keith suggested his coming."

"You must appreciate Gene's interest in my daughter."

He said again, "Oh, really! We both know that's an evasion. If you won't have him up here you won't. I shall advise you that my secretary is taking this inquiry down verbatim and that all or any part of it may later be used. This is simply another way of saying that anything—"

"I know. I do not want to seem rude, but I know, Mr. Heffernan."

"All right, then. Why did your husband come here, Mrs. Elser?"

"I'm sorry but I honestly do not know. I did not even know that he was living until I saw him in that room. And then he was dead."

"Why did you go to the room?"

"I—(Nan screamed and I heard Nan scream and I ran to the room and saw Nan with the gun in her hand.) "I don't know."

"Why did you scream when you got there?"

"Because of what I saw when I turned on the lights." (That's right, *I* screamed. It was *my* scream that brought Nan running, I brought the rest running.) "There was the general disorder—Robert lying on the floor—shot."

"Then you recognized him immediately?"

"No—not until Doctor Starr asked me whether I knew him."

"And still you did recognize that this strange man lying on the floor was dead?"

"Yes."

"And that he had been shot?"

"Yes."

"In other words, you were close enough to observe the bullet hole, and still you did not recognize him as your husband?"

"I didn't then. Not then."

"Your daughter joined you?"

"Yes. Nan heard my scream."

(What did he know? Had he questioned Nan? What had she told him?)

"How long were you and she together before the others came?"

"I could scarcely have been a matter of seconds."

"When did you raise the window? Before or after your daughter came?"

"Window?"

"Please, Mrs. Elser. You must place some credence in our efficiency. Your fingerprints were on it. They were not on it earlier in the day when the room was examined in connection with Parne."

"I remember about that now, Mr. Heffernan. It is really inconsequential. I felt faint. I raised the window for air and then closed it again."

"Before you screamed?"

"No, naturally afterward. After the shock."

"But before your daughter came?"

"Yes."

"We've tested it, Mrs. Elser, and it has been estimated that between your screaming and the arrival of Doctor Starr and Lorrimer Keith and Gene Forrest not more than eight or nine seconds could have elapsed. And you want us to understand that you screamed, you felt faint, so you opened the window and were revived and then you closed it again, all before your daughter arrived, all within the implausible short space of three or four seconds?"

"I'm afraid I must."

"Why did your husband come here?"

"You have already asked me that."

"Can you suggest any reason, even though you know of no definite one?"

"No, Mr. Heffernan."

"Would you prefer us to accept a statement from you that you opened the window to throw something out into the snow?"

"No—no, I felt faint. I've told you that too."

"People have the funniest notions about the concealing qualities of snow. They think a subsequent fall or a continued fall of flakes will cover all traces. Well, in some cases it does."

"Yes?"

"But there are ways. The snowfall since you opened the window has been negligible, Mrs. Elser. There's that to begin with. Then there was the light."

"Light?"

"Shaft, really. We took a spotlight and shafted it almost horizontally over the area covered by the window. It narrowed the field amazingly by showing the indentations and making them quickly obvious. We found this by digging." Heffernan took a gun from his pocket and placed it on the piecrust table beside their chairs. Lily looked at it. It looked like the gun all right, and the spotlight business did make sense. It irked her strangely to have to remain so stubborn, so willfully unseeing, but there was no other course. She could admit nothing, agree to no point whatever, without her whole defense crumbling and leaving, not her, but Nan naked to the state's attack.

"I understand your contention, Mr. Heffernan. I do not admit any knowledge of that gun, and certainly I refuse to change my statement that a feeling of faintness caused me to open the window."

"Just as you wish, Mrs. Elser.

He left the gun lying there for Lily to look at, in the accepted tactics of it being a disturbing factor to prod her sense of guilt and in the hope that it would help him swiftly to break her down. As the ax must fall he wanted to wield it quickly, to have his former deeply admired friend confess in toto her horrific sins and throw herself upon the mercy of the state, accept a lesser plea and languish for twenty-odd years at some penal tasks, but at least escape with her life. As he would then in turn escape from her ultimate and nerve-destroying shout when the death penalty would be imposed. He held no question as to Lily's guilt, but he did hope for palliative circumstances and he wanted to find them out.

"Let us go back, Mrs. Elser. Way back. To when you and your daughter came here to Laurel Falls."

"I've done so just now, Mr. Heffernan, to Doctor Starr."

"Then repeat it, please for me."

Lily did. She gave him the bones of the framework with their dates and ignored any of the flesh, which was the really important thing and consisted of her years of distress when she had suffered as a brutally deserted woman. Heffernan considered them briefly in silence.

"I feel better, Mrs. Elser. We return to a normal groove. I am accepting your statement as to the divorce and the legal declaration of your husband's death because both can be checked at their documentary sources. Frankly it spoils my thoughts on a motive. Equally frankly it presents me with a more unpleasant one."

"You will forgive me if I fail to follow you."

"It occurs to me that the coming of Parne and Hangaway and your first husband to this house begins to make sense. We have Parne's initial interest in the Sheraton secretary. We have your husband's search of the room which Parne occupied and in which he was killed. I refer to the slits in the mattress and the opened pillows, the general disorders of a search. Papers, documents of some nature naturally spring to mind. Equally so your documentary proofs of the divorce and the declaration of legal death also spring to mind. I suppose you kept them here, Mrs. Elser. Or are they at the bank?"

"No, I kept them here. Because of my early contention of being a widow I preferred to hold them privately."

"Where?"

"I have kept them since Mr. Elser's death in the Sheraton secretary."

"Well, we've searched it and there's nothing of their nature there. Or are there secret compartments?"

"No. There is a locked drawer for more private papers. I kept them in that."

"Yes, I know the drawer. It has been forced. By Parne, I imagine."

Heffernan frowned. He was deeply bewildered and puzzled. He forgot for a moment in his concentration on the problem the relationship that currently existed between himself and Lily, with himself a bloodhound baying slaveringly after this (once) delightful, delicate creature as she skipped with such pitiful indecision across her perilous and tipsy cakes of ice. His manner changed to one of a man who is having an impartial discussion about a knotty problem with a friend.

He said, "I suppose we must consider it that way, that Parne found them in the secretary and took them and that your first husband was looking for them when he was shot. Only why? Can't you see how foolish it is?"

Lily couldn't. She was beyond seeing anything much, that is, as to its folly or brightness, and a dreadful, passionate longing to go away someplace and lie down and sleep was betraying her again. She meditated about this absently, thinking it queer, because of all times it was right now when she should be lively and electric and in all ways on her mettle, ready with parry and thrust to beat off this important gnat who was bent on destroying her.

"In what way is it foolish, Mr. Heffernan?"

"Because they are not documents of source. Anybody could go to the place where you got your divorce and look it up in the official records, and it's stupid to consider that *they* could be done away with."

He looked for understanding in this now-impartial friend and saw none. Her lovely eyes with their deep shades of blue and violet seemed a touch out of focus and windowed with glass. He wondered for a scandalized moment whether she had been paying any attention to him at all or had just remained wrapped up in her glassy daze and throwing him mechanized in the manner of an intelligent automaton.

He said sharply, "The same thought holds true, of course, with the legally dead business. So why all this frantic to-do about getting hold of your copies?" An odd idea took shape in his mind and he stared at her strangely. "Why do you call that man Robert Warden, Mrs. Elser? Don't you know that his name is Worthby Haines?"

Lily's pale face grew paler as the blood left it slowly and she thought, becoming at once all awake: That's the name Mr. Hangaway asked Nan about. He asked her if she knew Worthby Haines, and Nan said no. He asked her how she had got wise to Worthby Haines. He asked her how much she had shaken him down for. He had said to Nan: "Haines is hard—as you know. He'd see to it that somebody wrapped you up in cement just as quick as he'd pick a daisy. You'd better turn the proof over to me."

"Worthby Haines? I'm afraid not, Mr. Heffernan. I have never known Robert otherwise than as Robert Warden."

"Were the divorce and the other papers issued under that name?"

"Yes."

"And the name Worthby Haines, Worthby Haines of Detroit, means nothing to you, Mrs. Elser?"

"Nothing. Absolutely nothing, Mr. Heffernan."

He seemed unbelieving and astounded that it should not, and Lily thought that Robert or (now) Worthby Haines must be a man of noted importance. She tried to imagine Robert, her earlier cruel and ferally exciting Robert, as being now a man of importance, with his hard and, she hoped, reasonably unique tendency toward putting people in cement.

A startled look of sudden shock spread over Heffernan's face.

"Mrs. Elser, why did you send your daughter to Detroit?"

"I didn't. I didn't send her. Nan herself suggested going. She won a design contest conducted by the *Detroit Free Press*. She is a graduate in fashion design. That is why Nan went to Detroit, Mr. Heffernan."

Lily tried with the very essence of her heart to have Heffernan believe this because so far as she knew it was true, and she wanted to make the truth of it so ringing that he would have to accept it. She watched the alarm fade from his face and his expression change to one of disgust and pity, like the look, she reflected, reserved for all the feet that ever were of clay.

He started addressing a jury, not Lily.

He said, "The roots of these crimes lie in this house, Mrs. Elser. They lie in those documentary proofs. But the tree and the branches spread over Detroit. Parne and Hangaway are shadowed by them, and so is the man whom you call Warden and whom I know to be Haines."

Lord, he thought, but this is silly. I'm talking to her as though I were summing up. She ought to throw me out of the house. She can't. She can't do a thing but sit there and listen to me, to my cheap pseudo-oratory, and hold her neck out until it pleases me to slice it with an ax. He was back to that image again, the bloodhound role no longer of use, because he had her. He had her right on the block. He wanted to apologize for his bombast but did not dare permit himself the least weakening into soft-ness. He took some notes from his pocket and studied them for a while.

He said to Lily, "A shorthand transcript wasn't kept the last time I questioned you, but this is approximately what you told me, Mrs. Elser. I shall ask you the same questions again and my secretary will take down your answers. Please consider them well, as you may care to answer differently than you did before."

"I feel certain that I shan't, Mr. Heffernan."

"This is about the way it went. I asked you what you did concerning Parne's room after he got here. You said you went up to it while he and Sheffield were putting his car in the garage. You checked the linen. You lifted his bags from the floor to the luggage stand. The only other time you went to the room was immediately after Hangaway had told you about the body. You then went up and stood in the doorway but did not enter the room at all. I guess that was about it."

"Yes. It still is, Mr. Heffernan."

"Wait please. I shall put the questions to you somewhat differently, and Mr. Minkle will take down your answers. When you went upstairs to check the room had Parne been in it as yet?"

"No, he did not go up until after he had put the car in the garage."

"Now in regard to his bags, Mrs. Elser. Sheffield has told me that he placed them on the luggage stand. You tell me that you did."

"I'm afraid that Sheffield is mistaken. Perhaps I am myself mistaken. The matter seems very unimportant. So very many more important things have happened."

"Still, if you will forgive me? Were the bags unpacked?"

"No."

"Why did you search them, Mrs. Elser?"

(Because I was looking for a gun or hot money or a case of dope, and later I searched them, looking for the letters he had written in the library and which might contain references which would connect him with Nan, and this later time I found the cabinet photograph of Nan which had been taken in Detroit. You can see how that proved that there *was* some-thing between them. Are pieces of cardboard carried away completely; or do they sometimes remain, and do the police examine the traps and the drains as a routine procedure in the expectation of finding just such incriminating things?)

"But I didn't search the bags, Mr. Heffernan."

Heffernan went off on a tangent. He said angrily, in anger at the entire situation, "There is this about a person's statements; there is this about the truth, about knowing anyone personally and believing him a truthful person. You catch him out in a lie, even in a little lie, but you know it to be a deliberate one. Everything else he says, everything he has told you before collapses. Surely you understand that."

"Of course I do."

"And still you tell me that you did not search the bags and that they were not unpacked. And still your fingerprints are all over the smooth leather case in which Parne kept his toilet articles, a case which had not been unpacked but which was inside his Gladstone bag. What in heaven's name do you want me to think, Mrs. Elser?"

"If you will give me one moment—"

"I will give you all the time you like."

Not that one moment or one year or one eternity would do any good. What was the use of a respite, no matter how long, if you were to spend it in this state of utter unliveliness—for she was back in *that* condition again—and were incapable of anything but the most febrile sort of fencing, because your head was asleep and all the rest of you was dead on its feet.

"As I have said, Mr. Heffernan, there were so many more important things which have intervened—but I must have lifted the bags to the luggage rack, not Sheffield—you both forget and imagine things easily after you've turned a century, and some people believe that Sheffield has—and the dressing case must have fallen out of the Gladstone when I lifted. I am certain that the bags were open. Mr. Heffernan. I can swear that the bags were open."

He looked at this puny effort and brushed it aside. What under the sun did she take him for? A complete chump?

"Do you know anything about blood, Mrs. Elser?"

"Blood?"

"About the four groups into which it's divided?"

"Yes, in a general fashion. You read so much nowadays about blood donors."

"The groups are called One, Two, Three and Four. Sometimes they are referred to as Group O, Group A, Group B and Group AB. It happens that Group AB is rare."

"Is it, Mr. Heffernan?"

He wanted to stick not one but a good many and long pins into her. "Parne's blood was of Group AB."

"Yes, Mr. Heffernan?"

"I shall ask you this, Mrs. Elser. While Parne was alive were you at any time in his room while he himself was in it?"

"No."

"Now after Parne was killed you tell us that you stood on the threshold of his room but did not enter it. I shall ask you did you in any fashion contact his body? I shall forget all former statements, Mrs. Elser."

Lily saw now where this was heading. It hadn't been simply blood which she had rinsed out down the sink but a rare and special kind of AB blood with which, surprisingly, Mr. Parne had been filled. Surprisingly because nothing else about him had struck her as rare. She said after several moments, coming up from nightmare depths like swimming up through smothering treacle to a surface which would even be worse, "Yes, I think I did."

"Just tell me about it. As you now remember it, Mrs. Elser."

"I think the shock, the fear at later finding blood on the sleeve of my negligee, I think that is what has kept me from mentioning this before."

"Yes, Mrs. Elser."

"I did go into the room. My memory continues to be confused because of the excessive faintness I felt at the time. I think I tried to determine whether Mr. Parne was still alive. The blood stained my negligee then."

"How?"

"How?"

"Yes, Mrs. Elser, how?"

"Why—by coming in contact with the wound, I suppose."

"My dear Mrs. Elser"—pins, even the longest of them, were too short and he wanted spikes—"Parne was on his back. He had been shot in the back. There was no wound of exit in his chest. There was no blood on his chest. What blood there was lay beneath him on the floor."

"Then—I must have put an arm beneath him."

"Yes?"

"To raise him up."

"Yes?"

"To see whether he was still breathing."

"Minkle!"

"Sir?"

"Find Miss Elser, please. Ask her if she will join us."

"Yes sir."

"No—not Nan, Mr. Heffernan. Ask me what you like, but please not Nan, Mr. Heffernan."

"Sorry, Mrs. Elser. Go get her, Minkle."

* * * *

Heffernan said, "It's about Detroit."
Nan said, "Yes?"

"And about your father."

"Yes, Mr. Heffernan?"

"I want you to tell me first about your father."

"But how?"

"Tell me everything you remember about him."

"But I don't. I don't remember anything."

"Miss Elser, you are young. We've both known each other casually for a good many years. I can remember seeing you as a very little girl as far back as the Mansion House. I've seen you grow. And—well, mature."

(She had, too, now that he had pinned the thought down with words. There was a riper look which had supplanted her general legginess and other awkward-colt effects, a sort of tightening up and smoothing out. All this on the surface, of course, and he imagined that the same process must have been also going on inside, otherwise she never could have got herself involved in this infernal mess.)

He went on a bit less paternally, "I'm telling you as I've told your mother that my job here is distasteful. It is especially so from the fact that I know both of you and have always liked you. I realize that the truth is hard, but I earnestly want you to appreciate that you will be doing yourself a kindness in the end by sticking to it." He added uncomfortably, as if wishing to make untrue a fact about which he had no doubts, "There is no escape."

Lily said, "Nan darling, would you like Gene to be up here with us?"

"Oh *no*, Mother. Why?"

"To advise us, dear. To advise us what to say?"

"Oh, *please* no, Mother. Honestly, Mr. Heffernan, the first thing I knew about Father, even about such people as fathers, was when Mother told me that mine was dead. I think I must have been about four or five then, Mother?"

"Yes, darling."

"Four or five." Heffernan made mental calculations. "Five—that would be the year, or rather at the end of it, when your mother obtained her divorce. You were told about that, of course, Miss Elser?"

Lily said sharply, "No! Nan has never known."

"But I did, Mother."

Lily looked blank and stunned. She thought: Nan has known about it all these years. She has known that her father was alive. She has said nothing. Never by any word has she indicated this knowledge. It was an affront, sort of, and verged on duplicity, a lingering duplicity that had obviously continued through adolescence right down to now. It occurred to her how right Nan was about the littleness with which they truly knew each other.

"Did your mother tell you about the divorce, Miss Elser?"

"No, Mr. Heffernan. I don't think either you or Mother appreciates how much a girl of five or six really knows. I think when people get older, I mean a lot older, that they forget about the time when they were five or six themselves, that they had thoughts and wants and feelings even then, really strong feelings, Mr. Heffernan, and that they could figure things out. They forget all that and simply—well, they make pets of boys and girls—like animals—"

"Darling!"

"It's *true*, Mother."

"You still haven't told me, Miss Elser. I mean about how you knew."

"That was perfectly simple, Mr. Heffernan. I simply saw the papers on Mother's desk and read them. I just wanted you to understand."

"Understand?"

"Yes, why I kept it a secret. Because I knew it was a secret of Mother's and I didn't want to *violate* it. I would dream and think about it, and I know now how young I was about it and how I dramatized it, how I thought of my mother as a tragic figure and how much it made me love her and how much—how much—"

This, thought Heffernan, is simply fierce. Even Minkle's lush eyes seemed damper than usual. As for Lily and Nan Elser, in an instant the two of them were likely to be dissolved, fused in the saltiest of floods, and his ax would fall through butter. He thought: I am as fit to be a district attorney as a marshmallow puff. He hadn't the faintest idea what such a thing was, but it sounded right.

"Miss Elser!"

"Yes, Mr. Heffernan?"

"Are you getting this, Minkle?"

Minkle gave him a moist nod.

"Did you also know that your father had been declared legally dead, Miss Elser?"

"Yes, I knew about that too."

"Now I want you to tell me, please, the real reason for your having gone to Detroit."

"Why, I won a contest—"

Heffernan deliberately forced himself to be rude. How else could you remain unmelted? He broke in on Nan impatiently with, "I know that. You won a contest conducted by the *Detroit Free Press* in fashion design and, being a graduate in fashion design, you went to Detroit and got jobs in fashion design on the strength of it. Why?"

"Why?"

"Yes, Miss Elser. You had a home here. Your friends are all here. Your mother was left alone here. Your mother who had but briefly been bereft" (there I go again!) "of her husband. You left her in that state of grief. Why?"

"My mother had also been left pretty penniless, Mr. Heffernan."

"Oh, come—really, please, I don't know what sort of commissions you made with your designing but surely, Miss Elser, they'd be drops in a bucket?"

"Nan, darling, really, dear, I never knew."

"There's a lot you've never known, Mother. I *will* tell you why I went to Detroit, Mr. Heffernan. I went there to get money. I went to get a lot of money."

Heffernan thought, now that the truth was at long last popping out at him: I know you did. I knew it, you poor, wicked, sweet, nice kid. (For she still *was* a kid, no matter how apparently a ripening one.) You vile accomplice.

"Make money by what means, Miss Elser? I take it you had other plans than just fashion design?"

"Naturally."

"Well?"

"I shan't tell you. I simply won't tell you, Mr. Heffernan. I've had one person despise me, and I simply shall not have you despise me, and I shall not have Mother. Or Mr. Minkle."

"Miss Elser."

"Yes?"

It was like water. You got your hands on something that looked solid and away it ran through your fingers. There was a bitter sort of comfort in knowing that you could put a stop to all such leakage by freezing it.

"How did you get onto the fact that Worthby Haines of Detroit was your father, Robert Warden?"

"I didn't."

"Your mother told you, didn't she?"

"Mother? But this is sheer madness, Mr. Heffernan."

"Please, Miss Elser, we're not dramatizing now. For God's sake, please realize how serious this is. Two men are dead. They have been killed. They have been murdered."

Nan suddenly stopped looking mature. She dropped her pitiful cloak of being a fallow and an efficient woman of the world and shriveled into a terrified child.

"Yes, I know."

"Oh, *Nan darling*."

"It's all right, Mother."

"Please, Mrs. Elser, I'm handling this. You ask me to accept your statement that you did not know that Haines was your father, Miss Elser, so I must do so. Will you also ask me to believe that you did not know Worthby Haines as Worthby Haines?"

"No, I knew him to be Worthby Haines. But I never *knew* him, Mr. Heffernan. I told Mr. Hangaway that I didn't know him, didn't I, Mother?"

"Nan!"

"Oh, so you told Hangaway that, Miss Elser?"

"Yes."

"I see."

He didn't see, of course, but the fact in a vague fashion seemed to fit, as any fact might fit in the obvious combine of Hangaway, Haines and Parne. And naturally the two Elsers.

He said, "Just what do you mean by the statement that you knew him but you didn't know him?"

"I didn't *meet* him."

"Your dealings with him were through Parne, then, or Hangaway? They were your go-betweens?"

"Nan—don't answer that, Nan!"

Heffernan slammed his clenched fist down on the piecrust table. It became no longer a table. He ignored the wreckage. He ignored everything but his great confusion and his hot, sudden anger. He ignored Nan. His hot, badgered eyes blazed directly at Lily, no longer lovely or a friend. A common murderess. "Here's my last question for the record, Mrs. Elser."

"Yes, Mr. Heffernan?"

"Get this carefully, Minkle!"

"Yes sir."

"Mrs. Elser, I have you on record for the following false statements. You opened the window on discovering Haines' body because you felt faint. A lie. You opened it to throw the gun out. You did not recognize the gun. But your fingerprints are on it. Now go back. You lifted Parne's luggage onto the stand. I believe, on the contrary, that Sheffield's statement is correct and that it was he who did so. You did not search Parne's bags. Your fingerprints are on the toilet-article case that was in his Gladstone, so you did search his bags. Now the blood."

"Please, I beg of you, Mr. Heffernan, I want Nan to go."

"I want her to stay. I repeat, the blood. Parne's blood. You stated you never entered the room after his death. His blood is on the sleeve of your negligee. So you tell us you lifted him up, by shoving your arm beneath his back, to see whether he was still breathing. Mrs. Elser, no child and, God knows, no jury would believe any stuff like that."

"Go, Nan darling—"

"Stay right where you are, Miss Elser. Mrs. Elser, I am giving you your last chance. I submit to you that you were not only in Parne's room after Hangaway had told you about finding the body but you were there *at the time of Parne's death!*"

"No—"

"I'm asking you to confess. I'm begging you to confess, Mrs. Elser."

"*No—*"

Heffernan's anger, his stuffed feeling of pumping blood, the hot ringing in his head, all dropped from him, leaving him a little shaken and weak. He shrugged faintly in a gesture of resignation which was, paradoxically, one of defeat at the wry moment of his indisputable triumph.

He said quietly, "After you shot Parne, Mrs. Elser, you wiped your fingerprints off the gun. You then dragged Parne's body to the hall door and placed his fingerprints on the two knobs. It was an awkward and an obvious job. The sleeve of your negligee became bloodied in that fashion. You dragged Parne back to the spot where he had fallen and then placed the gun in his hand."

His mouth had an ashy dryness and he tried to moisten it by swallowing before going on. "I will tell you how I know this. I have already explained to you that your fingerprints were clearly found on the smooth leather of his toilet-article case. Well, they were also dearly found on the smooth leather of his bedroom slippers, which came off his feet while you were dragging his body and which you put back on his feet after you had accomplished your stupid purpose." He ended almost lamely, almost apologetically: "As I have said, there is no escape."

Lily did not stir. She did not look at Nan. She could tell pretty well, without having to see it, how Nan would be looking. She hoped in her great despair that Nan would not speak, but in her heart of hearts she waited for the word from Nan that would save her, ready to deny it, to deny anything that Nan would say, but wanting the love and the feeling and the comfort of it even if only to remember during that interval when she would be, to all human purposes, alone. She waited just a little while.

And then she said, "How long will I have, Mr. Heffernan?"

He said miserably, "There is no special rush, Mrs. Elser. There's no earthly reason why you shouldn't stay here in your home while I'm arranging about the warrant. You can get your things in order." He started to hold out his hand and then drew it back, flushing hotly. "I'll come for you, Mrs. Elser."

Dull daylight grayed the windows, and a clock struck six.

* * * *

The kitchen was warm, with a cozy warmness from the range, and bathed in an eerie light from lamps which were absorbed and seemed vitiated by the strengthening gray of morning daylight through the windows.

Nan poured two cups of coffee and said to Gene, "Shall we have it black?"

"Yes, please. Black."

He meditated on the hideous quarter of an hour she must have just gone through to get that wrung look on her face.

Nan said, "Not even sugar?"

"No, thanks. Just black."

"Here."

"Thank you."

"I've read that the first effects of coffee are to make you drowsy, the way any warm drink will, and that it isn't for over an hour or so before the caffeine gets to work and peps you up."

"Really?"

"Yes. I read it either in a paper or in a book."

It must have been hell. But wasn't it coming to her, Gene reflected, when you looked at it impartially, with a man-of-the-world point of view? You elected your own role or roles in life, and if you failed to put them across you suffered the consequences. So just! So satisfactory! And so bitter. Fate felled you, regardless of the beauty, charm or sweetness of your shell. It simply ignored all that, and reached inside and twisted your middles. Life was a pendulum—nuts, he said to himself.

"Nuts," he said aloud.

"Gene!"

"Sorry. I was thinking."

"Well?"

"About you."

"Well?"

Scarcely conversation, this. But who wanted it? It chilled Gene to realize what he really did want. He wanted nothing else, no single thing on earth, but to take this creature, this designing tramp, into his arms and let her cry her eyes out against his chest. The folly of it appalled him and vigorously insulted his matured and, now added, worldly sense.

"I'll have some more, please."

"Certainly."

Nan poured coffee with fingers that quite rightly trembled, making the lip of the pot a castanet against the cup.

"I was thinking about your prospects." (Amazing that these words should be coming out, shoving a rude course up through all of his good worldly wisdom!) "I was thinking that the best thing you can do is to marry me and be damned quick about it."

"Why, you beast!"

"That's right."

* * * *

Lily was satisfied in the glass with the plain dark gray tailored tweed. She went out into the hallway. Its lights were still on, in competition with the sullen morning, and a uniformed policeman stared at her stonily for an instant and then shifted his eyes to an inch or so above her head. From the landing she saw Dr. Starr at the foot of the stairs, talking with another uniformed policeman. Lily waited until Starr seemed to have finished.

"Doctor Starr—"

"Oh—yes, Mrs. Elser?"

"Would you mind?"

He came upstairs and joined her on the landing.

"I am trying to set things in order, Doctor."

"Yes?"

"I had meant to ask you earlier whether you would be good enough to take a look at Delilah."

"Is she ill?"

"I don't know. She has the usual misery, which could cover anything. I'm a little worried about her. About her manner."

"Manner?"

"Yes. Sheffield and Nan and I went up to her room after Mr. Hangaway had gone. She apologized for wanting to stay in bed—with her misery—and her manner struck me as being queer. Will you come up with me now?"

"Of course, Mrs. Elser."

They went upstairs.

Lily rapped on the door and said, "Doctor Starr is with me. May we come in, Delilah?"

Several seconds passed before Delilah's voice said, "Please do, madam."

They went inside and Lily found the scene unchanged. The room was gloomily a little brighter, and the shadows from the bed lamp were gone. Delilah still was sitting up on the bed and clutching the bright pink nightgown tightly about her withered body.

"Good morning, Doctor Starr, sir."

"Good morning Delilah. Which misery is it this time?"

"Just a general all-around touch kind, Doctor, sir."

Starr went to the bed and felt Delilah's wrist, taking her pulse. His eyes widened sharply and it seemed to Lily, as she watched him, as if his body stiffened. He kept his fingers on the wrist for a full minute, saying nothing. Then he said casually, "What have you been eating, Delilah?"

"Nothing out of the ordinary, sir."

"Well, we'll see."

Starr looked penetratingly into the soft, blank darkness of Delilah's eyes. He gently rubbed a finger tip across her upper and lower lips.

He said, "Nothing to worry about. You might take this prescription downstairs if you will, Mrs. Elser, and ask one of the men to go to my office for it. Miss Wadsworth will give him the proper stuff."

"Yes, Doctor."

Starr took a prescription pad from his pocket.

"My writing is the usual unintelligible scrawl that is always attributed to medical men, Mrs. Elser. The worst thing about the libel is that it's true. Here's the proof of it."

He tore the sheet from the pad and handed it to her. A shock ran through Lily as she read:

> *Hangaway is in this room. Go outside and leave the hall door wide open. Do not summon aid. This is imperative.*

Lily forced her voice to be natural and calm.

"Doctor Starr will have you fixed up in no time, Delilah."

"Thank you, madam."

"I'll join you downstairs shortly, Mrs. Elser. I just want to take Delilah's temperature."

"Yes, Doctor."

Lily's eyes, as she walked toward the door, were conscious of the room: swiftly speculative even through her flash of terror as to where Hangaway could be hidden. The bed was angled from a corner, and Hangaway could be crouched behind the head of it, of course, and the door to the clothes closet was an inch ajar. Her nerves jangled as each step seemed bent on becoming a prelude to some swift and narcotic-conceived plan of destruction, some weapon beyond the rational mind with the forces of mania directing the attack. Her fingers shook as they closed about the door-knob. She opened the door to its fullest extent. She went outside.

Starr shook a thermometer down.

He said to Delilah, "Just hold this under your tongue."

"Yes, Doctor."

Starr was vibrantly conscious of the moment's menace. He knew his maniacal minds. To combat them you had to place yourself upon a comparable plane, matching oddity with oddity, thinking ahead if possible into that diseased morass where the very essence of bright cunning was bred. He favored behind the head of the bed as Hangaway's place of concealment. He judged that a knife or an ice pick from the kitchen would be pressed between the ornamental ironwork and through the pillow against which Delilah leaned, as a grim reminder of what an injudicious gesture or remark on her part could lead her to expect.

He took the thermometer from her mouth and put it in its case and back in his pocket, without looking at it and staring all the while at Delilah, sending his wave of thought into the dark pools of her knowing old eyes.

"Ninety-nine degrees. Well, that's nothing. I'd go light on food today, Delilah."

"I will, sir, Doctor."

"Just stick in the neighborhood of toast and poached eggs. Some tea."

"Yes sir, Doctor."

With quiet fingers he loosened the bedding which lay above her lap.
"Have you pains anywhere? Any aches?"

Delilah looked at him earnestly, inquiringly, seeking his lead.
"Well, sir—"

"How's the chest and the muscles in your back? Does this hurt?"

A strong arm slid behind her back; his other slid beneath her legs, and in an instant her withered fragility was gathered up, swiftly off the bed, swiftly out into the hallway, where he set her down and shut the door. He said to Lily who was standing motionless at the stairhead, "You can tell them to come up now, Mrs. Elser. Tell them to be quiet about it, and please suggest that a man be posted outside in case he jumps from a window."

"Yes, Doctor."

Starr held Delilah until she had stopped her fit of trembling.
"Go downstairs, Delilah."

Starr stood and looked steadily at the knob of the door. No sound came from within the room whatever. It was not a man, he meditated, who was in there but an elemental force, a power and a strength which were cunningly motivated by the obverse of logical reason. A hundred weapons lay at Hangaway's hand, even if you expected the probable one of the kitchen knife or the ice pick. The barrenness of an asylum cell exampled that: its lack of any weight or movable object or cutting edge or pointed thing with which to stab.

Starr's problem absorbed him. It did not deal with Hangaway. It dealt with Lily. He could himself, he felt, be a match for Hangaway, and the added odds of the other men in the house made Hangaway's capture or his death assured. Even a single tear-gas grenade would cover any of that.

But none of those things would cover Lily Elser.

There was this about Hangaway as Starr reviewed it: he mustn't be captured and so turned into a sullen mute; he mustn't be killed during any attempt at escape, and he mustn't be permitted to take his own life. He must be left and interviewed at ease. Starr moved several steps away from the door and closer to the stairhead, picturing in his thoughts a probable view of Hangaway who would now be crouched or standing in a speculative silence with an ear pressed against the door, a bemused finger resting perhaps on the home-shot bolt.

Heffernan headed the silent advance.

Starr motioned him to silence and brought his lips close to Heffernan's ear, whispering, "There is a bare chance that he may let me come in."

"Take this gun."

"No. It can't be done that way."

"He'll kill you. You should have seen him when he went berserk at the hospital."

"He won't go berserk if I can help it. He's got to talk."

"Talk about what?"

"The truth about why Parne and Haines were killed."

"What do you think he knows?"

"No one knows what he knows, not even himself. It's my job to find out."

"You're taking too great a risk. We'll sweat it out of him."

"You couldn't. This is a psychiatrist's job, not a policeman's. This is the time to do it. This moment might not come again."

"What's the difference? We've proved that Mrs. Elser shot Parne."

"I've just got hold of as good proof that she didn't."

"What is it?"

"It's in connection with the blood group—quiet—he's testing the handle of the door."

Slowly, in the hall's gloomy light, the knob revolved, went back, was still in the stillness that was broken alone by the sound of men breathing.

"There may be some noise," Starr whispered. "He may have a flash of violence, but don't come in unless I call. Keep everyone below the level of the head of the stairs. He'll take a look out into the hallway. Hurry."

Starr waited until the men had retreated down the stairs. He went to the door and rapped.

"This is Doctor Starr, Mr. Hangaway. Will you let me come in, please?"

"You and who else, Doctor?"

"Nobody."

"What do you want?"

"You, Mr. Hangaway."

"You must be crazy."

"Possibly. I think I can persuade you that there has been enough blood. Are you in any condition to talk rationally?"

"Aren't you being insulting, Doctor? Stand away from the door."

"Certainly, Mr. Hangaway."

Starr moved back and stood against the opposite wall. The door inched open, then opened wider. Hangaway was a pipe-like shadow against the dullish gray within. His large head turned upon Starr and then moved and examined the empty hallway to right and left.

"Come in, Doctor."

"Thank you."

They went inside and Hangaway closed the door, thoughtfully shooting home its bolt.

"I find that you interest me, Doctor."

"We mutually interest each other."

"Yes. Try that rocker. I understand that they're coming back again as collectors' pieces of virtu. Funny animals, men."

"Very funny. In fact, their humors are endless."

"You must think I don't know."

"Know?"

"That there are men outside. That they're stepping softly up to the door. That they're waiting for me."

"Oh, that."

"I want you to take a good look at me."

"All right."

"Look at my face. Look at my whole general appearance. Would you want me as a friend?"

"I don't know. But if I should your appearance would have nothing to do with it. It never does."

"You're wrong there, Doctor. It has a lot. I'm forty-seven, and about forty of those years have taught me."

"I'm afraid I still can't agree."

"Let me put it this way. I'll admit the matter is an obsession with me. Who are the malcontents in life? They're the ugly people—not your sort, because you haven't the kind I mean—but my sort, the type of ugliness which hints at, which verges on the repulsive. Look at your press pictures of the average communist or agitator or any sort of militant crusader. They're a proof of what I mean."

"I suppose your panacea for such discontent would be a blanket order on a plastic surgeon or a beautician."

Hangaway smiled thinly.

"Well, there's nothing so fantastic in that. My point is that ugliness is a positive handicap. People do not seek you out. They either ignore you or avoid you and make their voluntary contacts with people who are pleasant to look at. The inner soul, that inside shining goodness, is all tripe so far as I'm concerned."

"Yes, so far as you're concerned."

"Do you think I have none?"

"I think that you failed or were prevented from cultivating it."

"No. No, it would have done no good. I'm not a malcontent in the sense we've been speaking of. I belong to the other group of ugly people, the ones who use their handicap as a springboard to leap into power and success. But there is a drawback common to both classes, Doctor. We live alone."

"Yes, that is true enough."

"We're single people except for whatever companionship is put up for sale. We've our sycophants and our court jesters in ratio to our money or our importance, but we have no friends. It becomes our one great dread."

"Solitude?"

"Yes, Doctor. That's why I let you in here. You took away the nigger woman. I want company when I go."

"Aren't Parne and Haines enough?"

"They're dead already."

Starr smiled at the statement's simplicity.

"You're not going to die, Mr. Hangaway."

"I should find small pleasure in living behind bars, Doctor. I think our journey will be best."

"Your childhood is at the bottom of this."

"That's right. It was my face."

"It alone. You have a good many years left you in which to readjust yourself. I say that sincerely."

"I know you do."

"Just now you're at the apex of a pitch you've been working yourself up to during the past few days. Or has it been for longer than that?"

"It's been since the time the boys started getting wise to Haines."

"Do you mind telling me?"

"Not a bit. That jug's cracked. For me at any rate."

"I don't know Detroit very well. I suppose it all centers there?"

"Yes. Did you know much about Haines?"

"No, just the general outline which Heffernan has given me. Politics, influential in the state machine, wealthy, being groomed to run for Congress on a reform platform with the governorship in view—that sort of stuff, wasn't it?"

"That's right. The strong, fearless, attractive type. A man's man, a friend of the people. Still and always a friend of the people even though his wife is one of the richest and most socially prominent women in the state and his daughter is ranking debutante number one." A look of awe came over Hangaway's face. "When this thing breaks!"

"What, Mr. Hangaway?"

"Why, that the kid's illegitimate, of course."

"His marriage—"

"Marriage? He was a lousy bigamist. He married Gertrude Witstock two years before Mrs. Elser got her divorce. And the kid, the current Jennie Elspeth Haines, popped out on the nine-months dot."

"You speak of the boys…?"

"The opposition, Doctor. Lanner Compson and his gang, they've had a political strangle hold on the state for years."

"And they know all this?"

"No, they suspect something like it, but they've got no proof. They know it the way a lot of big stories are known but never break. Doctor, you would be astonished at some of the stuff that is simply waiting for the first public false step before it is cracked down on the heads of a lot of important men."

"I suppose that's true. You say the boys have no proof in this case?"

"That's right. Parne came here and got it, of course, but he's dead, and Haines himself is dead, which leaves me. It's a shame, Doctor. Do you know something? I think I'll get out of here. I'm not going to waste this. I can still take Mrs. Haines and the kid for a million. I can take her for every nickel she's got."

"That's a pretty big order, isn't it? It means killing me, killing Mrs. Elser and her daughter, killing seven or eight armed men. I think it's stupid to figure on it, Mr. Hangaway."

"I suppose you're right. It's a pity though. I don't like things to go to waste."

"You aren't being very clear about all this."

"Why aren't I?"

"Or possibly I'm a little dense. Possibly it's because I'm not accustomed to mixing with important men. What's plain to you seems a bit unreal to me."

"What things?"

"Well, Haines in Detroit, how Nan Elser entered into it, the Elsers here—you speak of the boys getting wise—what put them wise?"

"That's easy. Miss Elser's picture in the *Detroit Free Press* after she won the design contest did that. You could feel it run all through town: 'What's Jennie Haines doing winning a design contest? No, it isn't Jennie Haines. It's some girl called Elser from some town in Ohio called Laurel Falls. Well, would you believe it? You could take them for twins. But after all, everybody has a double. Look at the movie stars, at the doubles contests, at any prominent person. So forget it.' So people did forget it, Doctor. But the wise boys didn't. Not them."

"Why?"

"Any pelt has some value, Doctor, and a political pelt runs into real dough. I don't have to tell you that. And remember that once Haines started running for public office he was right out in front, all washed and combed, as a target for mud. Naturally they had dug back into his past. They traced it easily to two years before his marriage. That was when he first hit Detroit. He wasn't an ugly man, Doctor. He was one of the lucky ones."

"Yes, I could see that. He would be attractive to women, especially back at that age."

"Right. Young and dashing and gallant Worthby Haines, fresh out of the golden West. A smart boy."

"Just how, especially?"

"Because he announced San Francisco as his origin. Because he announced that his parents and every contact that could be authenticated about him were wiped out in nineteen-six during the earthquake and the fire; in fact, that the horror of it all upon his childish mind had made the whole thing practically a blank. That was very smart. You can not substantiate nor deny any statements by poking about in cinders."

"No, you can't."

"Well, it was always in the back of the boys' heads. It was so good it was too good. So when Miss Elser's picture broke in the press they didn't watch Miss Elser; they watched Haines."

"Of course—"

"Sure, you get that. Being a doctor."

Starr asked suddenly, "What does Mrs. Haines look like?"

"You're right. She's the general type of Mrs. Elser."

"That so frequently happens with some men, with their successive wives."

"Yes, there's every reason why the half sisters should look alike. The Haines girl is two years younger, of course, but she's lived harder. Honestly, Doctor, these debutantes!"

"They get over it."

"Sometimes. Well, there you are."

"I'm afraid I'm not. Not yet. What did happen in Detroit after Nan Elser's picture broke?"

"As I say, they watched Haines. Oh, he saw the picture all right, and so did Mrs. Haines and the daughter. The boys have Haines' chauffeur on the pay roll so there isn't much they don't pick up. Mrs. Haines just commented on the likeness and forgot about it. So did the girl, after some occasional chitchat about it among other girls in her set. It struck both of them as amusing but as very unimportant."

"But not Haines, of course. Haines knew."

"That's right. He fixed it to meet Miss Elser. Casually. Only the boys considered it wasn't casual. It spelled the first flicker to them and they knew they were onto something really hot. I don't know what happened at that meeting. I don't even know whether they actually met. All I know is that both of them were at the same cocktail party one afternoon. A big party. I had my own ideas."

"What were they, Mr. Hangaway?"

"I like to look at all angles, Doctor. I figured from the other end: that maybe Miss Elser had come to Detroit on purpose to put the bee on Haines. You see, the thing that held the boys up from the start was that they didn't know positively what Haines' name really was. They considered it might be Elser, because they didn't know right away that Mrs. Elser had remarried and that the daughter had legally taken the name of Elser. They got a girl to contact Miss Elser easily enough, but all she could find out was that there was a Mrs. Elser in Laurel Falls, a widow, and that Nan Elser's father was dead. Then the boys put Parne on it."

"Just who was Parne?"

"He was a disbarred counselor who knew his way around. They used him a lot. Personally I always thought he was overestimated. He lacked finesse. His usual method for getting the dope on a woman was a cross between the chief suspect in a horror film and a ham juvenile, with a good deal of lurking behind the arras. He certainly fancied himself, that boy."

"Why did they use him then?"

"Because he got results no matter how crudely he got them. Then they'd get a laugh out of him too. But the women wouldn't. Usually they'd be worried into fits by all of his hamming and ready to come across with whatever dope he was after on his first serious pass. I know he started his usual routine with Miss Elser. He began to flush her out, make her lose jobs, almost black-list her. He'd show every now and then and let her get a look at his face with one of its most significant expressions. Lord, *what* a ham, Doctor. I guess Miss Elser dreamed about it in nightmares."

"How do you know all this, Mr. Hangaway?"

"Well, I came into it around then. Right after the boys hired Parne for the job Worthby Haines hired me."

"Why?"

"You don't get to be where Haines got by being a dumb bunny, Doctor. He knew what was going on. He knew they had sicked Parne on Miss Elser, so he sicked me on Parne."

"You said a moment ago that you were doubtful about Miss Elser, that you considered she herself might have come to Detroit to blackmail Haines."

"That's right. I knew definitely she was out for dough, but I figure now it was just the smalltime stuff of trying to lead one of the money boys up to the altar. I figure she must have doped Parne out as a bouncer for one of the First Families."

"Why were you in doubt at all about Miss Elser's purpose if you were in Haines' employ? Why didn't you know?"

"Listen, Doctor. When you work for a man like Haines you know only what he tells you and you do only what he tells you to do. Miss Elser and fifty other people might have been trying to throw their hooks into him and he wouldn't tell me about it or anybody else about it unless he had a purpose to. My job was Parne and just Parne."

"Just what kind of a job? Or do you mind?"

"Not a bit, Doctor. It all centered around Haines' real name. They had found out by then all they could, in general, about Mrs. Elser, about her coming here to Laurel Falls around the same time that Haines showed in Detroit and about her calling herself a widow, Mrs. Robert Warden. You can see what a job it would have been."

"To do what, Mr. Hangaway?"

"First they couldn't be sure that Warden wasn't just a name which Mrs. Elser had picked out, to cover whatever it was had happened before she got here. And even if Warden was the right name it would mean the impossible feat of checking every divorce record for years in the name of Warden or Haines all over the country. Absolutely impossible, Doctor."

"Yes, of course."

"They felt Mrs. Elser might have the documentary records here in the house or in town or else that Parne could get the information from her by his delicatessen tactics. Once they got her copies or the dope from her they could then check the records at their source. That's why Parne came here."

"And you, Mr. Hangaway?"

"Haines gave me twenty thousand dollars with which to buy Parne over to our side. If Parne couldn't be bought—which is a laugh—or if he shoved the ante up too high I was to use my judgment. That meant killing Parne and getting busy on the Elsers."

"You didn't kill Parne."

"I know I didn't." Hangaway's bright eyes grew speculative with interest. "Do you know who did? *I* know."

"Haines killed him."

"That's right. How did you dope that out, Doctor? They've got Mrs. Elser sewed up and in the bag."

"If Haines were alive he could be sewn up in the same bag."

"But how?"

"Mrs. Elser did a lot of foolish things because I believe she felt her daughter was involved."

"Sure, but how do you pin it on Haines?"

"Blood."

"Yes?"

"Parne had Group AB."

"Rare."

"Yes. Mrs. Elser got some of it under the sleeve of her negligee while she was holding up Parne's body and putting his fingerprints on the door-knobs. Do you know the layout of the hallway outside of the room Parne occupied and outside of the one you yourself used so briefly?"

"Yes."

"There is a shallow alcove, if you remember, at the end of it. It has a door opening into a linen closet."

"Yes, I know."

"That enters into my reasoning, but first about blood. Consider Haines. He was shot through the head. It was the type of wound that bled a little but not excessively. There were the normal blood trickles on his face, but there were also several bloodstains on the white cuff of his shirt. It bothered me as to how they could have got there, and there was the further fact that they were not fresh. You will understand my interest in Mrs. Elser's welfare, that I wanted to leave no possible contradiction unchecked?"

"Certainly, Doctor. For a town like this she is very okay."

"Well, Haines' blood checks as Group O, whereas the bloodstains on the cuff of his shirt have just been identified as Group AB—that is, Parne's. Which places Haines as well as Mrs. Elser upon the scene of Parne's death."

"Any D.A. could still make it stick on her in spite of that."

"There is more. I have just finished looking. There is another stain. It is on some linen in the linen locker where I believed Haines waited, resting his hand and freshly bloodstained cuff on the linen, after he had shot Parne and searched the body and while Mrs. Elser was doing her stupid and tragic act in Parne's room. Mrs. Elser could not have transferred that stain from the sleeve of her negligee. It is on one of the higher shelves, where a man's hand would reach naturally for a rest and where his cuff could leave it on the linen. Mr. Hangaway, Haines had hired you to do his work for him. Why did he come here himself?"

"Doctor, who can tell about a man like Haines? They get so smart they get too smart for their own good. This business meant the ruin of his career if not of his life. He hired me, yes, but why should he take a chance? He would want to check me, if possible, with his own eyes. Then you have the blizzard."

"Blizzard?"

"Sure, the jams, the road conditions, all of it. Haines trailed me from Detroit, only I stopped off at that filling station and he passed right by it in the blinding snow and reached here alone."

"Of course—"

"Sure. He parked his car in town and walked here to the house and looked in the living-room window and saw Parne at the secretary. Then he simply tapped on the window. Parne recognized him and maybe got scared stiff and maybe saw a chance for a swell shakedown. Anyhow, Parne pocketed the pearl-handled gun that was in the secretary and opened the front door and let Haines in. They went upstairs to Parne's room, and Haines got tough and Parne pulled the gun on him, and Haines just took the gun away and shot him."

"Why didn't Haines leave the house at once and start back for Detroit?"

"Because Parne didn't have the papers. Haines tapped on the window before Parne found them, and Parne was just putting on a bluff. So Haines had to stick around here until he could get the papers himself. He used the rafters in the attic."

"When did he get the papers?"

"Well, what with the cops about he didn't get a real chance until I came here from the hospital and knocked out that pretty boy on guard at the front door. He took his time going through Parne's room, and then he came downstairs and found them in the secretary."

"Where were you?"

"That was just when I had finished with Mrs. Elser and her daughter and that shine and while I was coming downstairs myself. Naturally I wanted to talk it over with Haines, and I had the cop's gun, so we went back upstairs and into Parne's room and talked. I told him how I had him for bigamy and for murder and we talked for quite a while, but it was no use. He made a jump for me and I had to shoot him and take any chances for a real shakedown with either the boys in Detroit or with the widow and the illegitimate girl direct. You were downstairs at the time with some other guy, Doctor, and Miss Elser was just saying good night and coming upstairs, so I came up here and got behind the nigger woman's bed. I kept her quiet with this."

Hangaway took an ice pick from his hip pocket and tapped it gently against one pipe-like knee. He said to Starr very quietly, "How did you know that I was here in the room, Doctor?"

"Because you had planned to leave it, to make your escape."

"Yes."

"You had taped Delilah's wrists and her lips with adhesive tape."

"Yes."

"When Mrs. Elser knocked and asked whether she and I could come in Delilah didn't answer for several seconds. During that time you removed the tape and got behind the head of the bed."

"Yes."

"Surely it is obvious, Mr. Hangaway? When I felt Delilah's pulse I also felt the sticky glue which remained from the tape about her wrist. I felt it also over her lips."

Hangaway shook his head slightly and sighed. A flash of sudden irritation made his fingers tremble.

"Just think, Doctor—because of a little thing like that. All of the trouble for nothing."

"I hope you are including in it the rather tragic amount of trouble that came to the Elsers."

"Them? Smalltime stuff, Doctor. Just a couple of little people who happened to get in the way."

"Yes, I suppose you do look at it like that. That Haines looked at it in that way, and the boys did too."

"Why not?"

"Well, thank you, Mr. Hangaway. Are you ready to come with me now?" Hangaway looked at Starr steadily for a while. It was impossible to read a single thought behind the dull smoky glaze which was masking the former glitter in his eyes. He flicked the ice pick impatiently in his fingers.

"You're coming with me, Doctor. Not me with you."

Starr took a small metal case from his pocket.

"You said that I interested you, Mr. Hangaway. I think that this will interest you even more than I do myself." He opened the case and spilled a hypodermic needle and a vial of pellets onto a table. "Morphine."

Hangaway grew rigid and sat very still. Slowly the ice pick dipped and dropped, ignored, from his twitching fingers. He gave a small strangled cry that was more animal than human and started to walk slowly toward the table.

Starr unbolted and opened the door.

"All right, gentlemen. You can come in."

* * * *

Lily took off the tailored gray. She did not want to see the suit again, with its reminder of the torment of the past few hours. She wondered about the house, too: whether it were spoiled for her forever or whether time and the sunlight of succeeding days would cleanse it of its bitter memories. They were too vivid and much too close upon her now to tell. This room with the foot of the bed on which Hangaway had sat—the slipper chair—the window at which Heffernan had stood—the place where Sheffield, beaten, had crumpled and dropped—each step with its wrenching reminder.

This basin in which pink had spread while Nan—and that—and in the mirror, standing in the doorway, just as she had then been standing in the doorway, was Nan.

"Mother—"

"Darling?"

"It's stopped snowing, Mother."

Lily dried her hands, wondering what move to make, what word to say, and then she thought: That's the trouble. She's my child. I've had to guard each word, each move, each minute of the past long days, and I'm still thinking in that groove. She's my child, and no words or gestures any longer matter, because there can't be any wrong ones any longer. We've been frugal, both of us, with the things that really count.

Lily put the towel down and started to hold her hands out. But again, with vivid cruelty, it was the night, and they dropped to her side, and the marble of the basin was cold against them. Nan moved a hesitant step and was closer.

"I'm so glad about Gene, darling."

"I've been an awful fool, Mother."

"No, you haven't, Nan. Neither have I been. Things have to hurt you before you can cure them."

"Gene thinks it will be all right if we don't wait for so awfully long. Do you?"

"I think whatever you do. I always shall think that way, Nan."

Nan's fingers touched her arm, warm, melting little spots of feeling which reached straight back through the years leaving Lily Nan and Nan a child once more, cradled against her, with their futures blank to write on. And everything was fixed. Tightly and so simply, just by this hanging onto one another, making up for the past and sealing the coming years. If you could imprison a moment under a clear glass bell... Lily thought: I'm being foolish, because I'm happy and because I'm tired and because we're close now. Close. Even when she's married to Gene we will be. She's never been so truly mine.

Delilah rapped and came in.

"I have arranged some breakfast, madam."

"Thank you, Delilah. We'll be right down."

"It has stopped snowing, madam."

"Yes," Lily said, "I know."

Lily put on a house dress of Nile wool, feeling younger and refreshed and more forgetful with each added second that passed. She went with Nan out into the hallway and thought it amazing how pallid its special memories were so quickly growing. How bright the tense whiteness of the morning made the hall below, with Lorrimer waiting stolidly down there in the bright white pool.

"I hope you don't mind," he said. "We all thought we'd like to eat. You haven't got rid of us. We're all here."

"I suppose there's nothing I can do about it."

"Nothing at all. Just be graceful and pretend you're glad of it. I understand felicitations are in order, Nan. It's about time."

"Thank you, Mr. Keith."

"I won't have it. Say Lorrimer the next time you speak to your mother's imminent husband. Go ahead—say it."

"Lorrimer."

"That's better. You're a grown girl now, and it's time you had some manners. Are we going to stand here all day, Lily?"

"I'd like to, Lorrimer."

"So would I. Beat it, my good child, for a minute—will you, Nan?"

"Yes, Lorrimer."

They stood for a while looking after her, and Lily said, "I'm thinking of the other one, of Nan's half sister, and the mother. Must they be told? Is there anything that can be done, Lorrimer?"

"It has been, Lily. They're not to know. Chance brought them to this house in refuge from the storm, Haines and Hangaway and Parne, and that's the story. There'll be no trial because Hangaway is admittedly insane. He'll never talk. Starr gives him just a little while to live."

"I saw her photograph, you know. I thought her Nan."

"You thought too much, you sinful woman."

"I'm not. I'm just a wreck."

"Nothing that a good overhauling won't fix."

"You're sure?"

"Yes."

"*Lorrimer...*"

"Lily—Lily—Lily."